GRANDMA'S PILLOW

Published by Cynthia K. Schilling, Champaign, IL.

Printed on acid-free paper.

Cynthia K. Schilling, Champaign, IL 61821
2015

First Edition

DEDICATION

To my husband Pat, for your love, encouragement, and the precious gift of time without which this book could not have been possible.

To my wonderful sons, step-daughter, son-in-law, and grandchildren—Joe, Jake, Emily and Mike, Maddie, and Will.

Each of you are a true blessing—my heart is forever full.

IN MEMORY OF:

Karen Hunt, whose gift for storytelling will forever outshine us all. You were the Angel who helped make this novel complete.

"When in doubt, look up."

Lowell Hunt, who reminded us to always watch the sunsets, and to Lindsey Helfers for her beautiful insight and description of the white butterfly.

ACKNOWLEDGEMENT

I give a special thank you to my good friend, mentor, and romance author, Taylor Nash. Your help, faith, guidance, and unfailing positive energy were the force and strength enabling me to write this book. Words of gratitude will never be enough for the abundant amount of time and effort you've given towards the completion of *Grandma's Pillow*. I offer you my deep heartfelt admiration and thanks. You were right, what a journey!

An extraordinary amount of thanks also goes to the following for their time and support in the production of *Grandma's Pillow*. Each of you helped make this novel complete.

Tillie DuBois	Cindy Line
Cathy Gorman	Mary Sigler
Becket George	Lauren George
Patti Kortkamp	Patty McFaddin

Thank you to Ann Halstead for her creative insight to this story. It was a blessing to reignite a friendship begun many years ago. It only took a spark...thanks, B.B.

Finally, to Christy S. Terry, thank you for your beautiful illustration of Grandma Rosie, Emmy, and Joy. Your vision captured each of them perfectly.

GRANDMA'S PILLOW

Cynthia K. Schilling

PROLOGUE

Present

Joy Miller was babysitting her new granddaughter, Kimberly, alone for the first time. Bending her head towards the small new life, puffs of the baby's soft breath brushed her nose, and the scent reminded her of a fresh picked white orchid.

The old rocking chair creaked. The baby slept peacefully swaddled in her arms. She was absorbed by the soft perfection of this new young soul now part of her, enchanted by her gentle features, focusing on her small cheeks the color of fresh blossomed pink roses. She gently outlined each small finger with her own, enamored by the tiny, unique creases formed on every knuckle, and brushed the curly blonde wisp of hair away from her delicate forehead.

This child was a new birth, a legacy, an assurance life would continue. She was overwhelmed by a depth of love even deeper than she remembered when she held her own child for the first time. She whispered to Kimberly her lullaby.

Close your eyes sweet baby girl,
  the world awaits your task.
Beyond life's simple dreams for now,
  high above, yet in your grasp.

Your outstretched arms won't reach them yet,
  the years will bring you near.
Soon your own sweet lullaby,
  will be told to those loved dear.

For now your world is simple,
  there is no need to rush.
Your sweet love given without a word,
  is felt within the hush.

The lullaby always offered a reminder to experience all the glorious adventures life had to offer. She prayed Kimberly would live her own dreams.

Most importantly, she wanted to pass on lessons of life that her own Grandma Rosie had taught her. Leaning carefully forward, she slowly pulled the worn white pillow that supported her back and set it on the opposite side of her lap so the pillow was in her granddaughter's view.

She glanced at the baby and back at the pillow. "Grandma's pillow," she whispered softly. She remembered her grandma's wide assortment of colorful ruffled pillows and the creative stories each of them held. A tear rolled down her cheek. She leaned her head against the rocking chair. Memories flooded in of Grandma Rosie and the unique way she used pillows to teach some of life's greatest lessons.

CHAPTER 1

*Live your life in a forest and
you will find your way through.*

June 1963

"I still can't believe she's ours. She's more perfect every day," the proud father, Sean Miller, remarked to his wife, Emmy. "Is that even possible, honey?" He scooted closer to her on the couch. They had brought their newborn daughter, Joy, home from the hospital a few days ago. Weighing six pounds and seven ounces, she was the spitting image of him. Her soft, thick brown curls echoed his; each strand sprawled across her head reaching one ear to the other.

The early summer heat coupled with the thickness of his hair sent beads of sweat running down the sides of his face. He didn't stir to wipe for fear he might miss the opening of her soft blue eyes, a reach of her tiny hand for him to place his oversized finger, or a glimpse of her anticipated smile. It was obvious over the past few days he was in love with two women: his wife, Emmy, and now his precious Joy.

"You two going to stare at her again all day or are you going to have some lunch? I've called out twice. Now hand me that precious jewel and go eat your sandwiches before I feed them over to little Fairway," Grandma Rosie threatened.

Grandma Rosie recently came to live in Cherry Grove with her daughter Emmy, and son-in-law, Sean. Her husband, Charles, had passed away and running a

3

farm, though small, on her own had become too much to handle. After much deliberation and despite her deep personal attachment to her Midwest home, she broke up housekeeping.

During the winter months she'd visit her sister Lelia in Arizona. It was always quite a journey for Grandma Rosie when she boarded the train to travel out west. The trip would take two full days before she arrived at her destination.

Grandma Rosie never minded the trip nor did she ever complain. She appeared to have found solace in what was now reality, and expressed gratitude to Sean, Emmy, and Lelia for providing their homes to live out her years. Little did she know how important that decision and her presence would be for her special granddaughter, Joy.

Fairway, a two-year old white toy poodle, ran into the room making his way between his mother-in-law's two planted feet, almost knocking her over.

"Oh no you don't little felly. You get on back to the kitchen, your food's waiting for you in your bowl." Rosie stopped him in his path, picked him up as his four small legs continued their running motion in midair, turned him around and headed him in the opposite direction.

"Go on now you two. I need some alone time to get to know my new granddaughter," Rosie firmly stated.

Sean stared at Rosie as if she had sentenced them to a year of child separation. Reluctantly, he took Joy, swaddled in Emmy's arms, and handed over their precious new bundle. No parents had ever felt prouder or more protective.

"Now look you two, you're not leaving the country. You're just going in the next room to nourish your bodies for goodness sakes, now get, both of you."

"Thanks, Mom," Emmy chuckled. "I don't know how we would've gotten through these past few days without you."

He gently held Emmy's arm, helped her up and together slowly walked into the kitchen. He knew Emmy remained tired after her many hours of labor delivering Joy. Thank goodness the few days spent at the hospital helped her regain some strength for the tireless activities now centered on their newborn daughter.

Unfortunately for him, summer was his busiest time at work with long hours in the outdoor summer heat. He was grateful his mother-in-law could be here to help. She had a hidden knack for taking care of adults and children in ways inconspicuous to most. But in this case it was obvious; Rosie was over the moon in love with Joy and he knew she would cherish the months ahead with her only grandchild.

Later that evening Rosie finished up the dinner dishes, a task she never minded. She often teased it gave her time to reflect on what she had, and in rare cases hadn't, accomplished that day.

Emmy had fallen asleep upstairs early, catching up on her needed overdue rest. He was at peace in his oversized, red, easy chair in the living room while holding little Joy, humming a sweet lullaby. Her small eyes were shut and tiny hands fell open on top of her pink, crocheted blanket while she lay asleep and secure in his arms.

He could barely soak in the sight of this precious gift and questioned if this new chapter in his life was truly real. How could anything this perfect be his? Out of all his successes in life, this child would forever outshine each one.

"My precious little princess," he whispered into the silence.

A sudden crack of thunder vibrated throughout the house. He anticipated raindrops would follow. He hadn't watched the daily weather forecast, something he normally kept track of due to the nature of his job. The week's special homecoming made everything else, including the weather, insignificant.

A flash of lightning and another crack of thunder startled him in his sunken chair. He glanced down at Joy who was sound asleep in his warm arms despite the weather's rage.

An overwhelming sense of concern encompassed him; he lowered his head to his daughter's chest to confirm her heartbeat. Holding her tight made him feel secure, as Joy must feel wrapped inside his arms. Her abounding and innocent love would forever keep him warm. He hoped and prayed he could provide as much—and more—for her in the many years ahead.

The phone rang in the adjoining dining room. Rosie's hurried footsteps upon the wooden hallway floor indicated she'd answer within seconds. She always ran a tight ship whenever she visited.

"Hello, Miller residence."

He continued to stare at his daughter and smiled when she scrunched her face while she dreamt.

"Just a minute, Chris, I'll get him."

Unfortunately, Chris' call meant something had probably happened at the club. Maybe a circuit had been hit or one of the links was flooding again, a problem he often took care of after a significant amount of rain. A new drainage system had been on the ground's request list for the past three years. Flooding would continue to be a problem until a new system was in place, but the club members saw it otherwise, and supported the construction of a new snack bar instead. "I'd rather golf than eat," he often said under his breath, frustrated at the many endless meetings.

He reluctantly yet carefully stood up with Joy swaddled in his strong arms as Rosie came around the corner.

"Sorry, Sean, it doesn't sound good," Rosie remarked.

He guardedly handed the bundle over to her, and scratched his head while he strolled to the phone bench to sit down and talk with Chris. He was tired from the past few weeks. The thought of going to work tonight was the last thing he wanted to do. Yet, he knew they depended on him, sometimes too much.

"I'll be there as soon as I can. Thanks, Chris."

He sensed what his mother-in-law's thoughts would be before he set the phone down and stood up. They were quickly confirmed when he walked around the corner. Another loud crash of thunder reverberated.

"Now, Sean, you're not thinking of going out in this storm? Wait a few minutes 'til it has passed. It's getting dark, dearie, and it's too far of a drive this time of night. Use your head, jus' listen to that wind blowing," Rosie preached.

She was right. The wind was unusually strong. It was for that reason he had to confront the problem at the club. It was his responsibility, just like Joy.

"I have to go, Rosie. One of the old oaks near the clubhouse has fallen and brought a power line down with it. An electrical work crew is on their way, but all the circuits are out. Chris hasn't been able to get the power back on.

"We can't go without power long out there; too many items in the kitchen will go bad. Besides, if this rain doesn't let up, I'll have to go check on the grounds anyway. It shouldn't take long. Preventive medicine is the best medicine, right? Isn't that what you always say?"

Gritting her teeth, she showed half a smile. She hated when he quoted her. Rosie always seemed to have a saying about everything, and he enjoyed giving back her own digs when he could.

He loved his mother-in-law dearly. Her final decision to sell the farm after working the land for forty years alongside her husband made his heart ache. After Charles passed almost a year ago, he agreed with Emmy, Rosie continuing to work the farm was simply out of the question. Selfishly, his thoughts were at ease knowing what a tremendous help she'd be with Joy in the coming months ahead.

"Are you comfortable taking care of Joy until I get back?"

"You don't even have to ask, Sean. You know I am." Rosie didn't hesitate for a moment before she responded. "Don't you worry a dickens about us, we'll be right here when you get back. Right little Joy Lou?"

Rosie glanced down and smiled one of the biggest smiles only a grandmother could give. She commented earlier having a granddaughter was like raising Emmy all over again. Although she agreed Joy looked like Sean, she concluded the baby most definitely had her daughter's smile.

"Thanks, Rosie. I'll peek in on Emmy before I leave in case she's awake and let her know I'm leaving. If not, she'll never know I was ever gone. I'm glad she fell asleep early tonight."

8

Fairway sat at his feet, tail wagging faster than a ragtime beating metronome.

"Okay, I suppose you can come too, but you have to promise to be good, or you'll have to stay in the car."

He gave Rosie one last glance. She held his daughter close, smiling down at her. Rosie's eyes had seen such hard times and yet continued to convey love and approval without a single word being uttered. Three generations were living within his household now—Rosie was the alpha—Joy the omega. There was a quiet moment when she caught his stare and smiled.

"I'll be back as quick as I can," he whispered. He bent down and gently kissed his daughter one more time on her soft forehead.

"Goodnight my little princess, sleep well. Look for me in your dreams. I love you."

His yellow Firebird sped down the street followed by a loud rustle of wind that swept high above the trees.

The swiftly moving windshield wipers barely cleared the pounding raindrops. He cautiously made his way down the winding road that led to the Cherry Grove Country Club.

He'd worked there since high school doing various fix-it jobs. His six-foot-two build had always been an asset when anything out of reach needed quick repair.

After years of hard work and dedication, he was now the superintendent. It was essential he get there quickly to prevent further damage to the club, or, heaven forbid, the course. The raindrops pounded the pavement while he began his descent down Mammoth Hill, as the locals called it, and final curve before reaching the club.

"Are you doing all right, Fairway? We're almost there boy."

It didn't take much to get Fairway excited. He especially loved car rides and sat in the front seat eagerly looking out the window. He often wondered what Fairway thought as they quickly passed wooded trees and farmhouses. His tail wagged, excitedly attentive.

Off in the distance above the hidden tree line, flashing red and yellow lights reflected off the darkened sky. He hoped seeing trucks from the electric company meant they had already completed the repair on the downed wires. If they had, it would truly be a miracle.

Did I just call that a miracle? No, my miracle is safe and asleep. Her lullabies await me at home.

He quickly turned his attention back to the road. His vision froze on a large, brown image, silhouetted against the hammering rain. The figure posed motionless in his path. He swerved to avoid the frozen obstacle.

A resounding clap of thunder detonated above him drowning out his piercing gasp for breath. Before he could brake, the car crashed through the darkened guard rail, his arms and hands instinctively flying up to guard his face. A massive streak of yellow descended from the road down the side of the endless hill. He searched to regain direction and control. His arms were knotted and numb; his body twisted, wedged between the seat and wheel as the car continued to dive. Stabbing pains brushed both cheeks, the catastrophic roar of glass shattered around him. Fighting the darkness of subconsciousness, he mentally searched for a calm vision. He uttered words he prayed wouldn't be his last.

"Em-my."

He was trapped. The fight would soon be over.

Please, not now, not yet.

"Joy...."

A black tire bounced freely ahead as the severed Firebird continued to roll down the rock lined hill, finally crashing into the cement embankment below. Black smoke encircled a deafening silence. A resounding clap of thunder turned reality and life from moments ago into sudden and complete darkness.

Time held its breath in tribute.

High above the rubble, the image stood on the sodden road quiet and serene, deciduous antlers lowered as if bowed. Its frightened body shivered within its large frame. Without consequence, the four-point prince disappeared slowly into the nearby woods. Virile, unhurt, unharmed.

CHAPTER 2

Love is free.

June 1968

Joy Lou Miller woke up earlier than usual on a bright sunny Saturday morning. The five-year-old crawled out from beneath her soft pink and white princess comforter and ruffled white sheets. Her toes barely touched the floor. She immediately put on play clothes she and her mother had laid out the night before.

"Good morning, sunshine. It's a beautiful day, what are you going to do with it?" Her mommy walked into her warm, sunlit bedroom and propped her hands on her hips.

"Do you need some help, honey?" Mommy asked.

No, she would do it herself. Her outstretched arms, lost within her t-shirt, fought to find their way out.

"Thummer clotheth are eathy, Mommy. Do you want to know why I think thummer clotheth are eathy?" She paused, waiting impatiently for her mommy to answer. Their eyes met and silently held a stare. She wasn't going to say another word until her mommy repeated the question in full. It was a battle of wills and after gazing into her mommy's eyes, she knew she'd reign triumphant.

"All right, Joy...."

As though she knew she was wearing on her mother's patience, she took a deep breath. Her mommy would eventually surrender to the troops which were made up of one strong willed five-year old.

"...why are summer clothes easier?"

Her excitement could barely be contained; her bright blue eyes sparkled in anticipation of her answer.

"Becauthe, Mommy, all you have to remember to put on are thirtth, thortth, and thoeth. I dreth fathter than thuperman in the thummer."

She gave Mommy a quick peck on her cheek, skipped out of her bedroom, down the stairs, through the kitchen, and out the back screened door, letting it slam behind her. She hopped down five steps, counting each one out loud, and stopped at the entrance to what she considered her own private world where she fought dragons, climbed mountains, swung from trees, made dirt stews, built sand houses, and sang in her own imaginary choir. This was her universe—her backyard.

Stopping at the end of the steps, she scouted out her path. She squinted from the sun, its warmth caressed her lightly freckled face. Closing her eyes tight, she inhaled the sweet fragrance of lilacs that wafted from a distant bush. A light breeze moved through her long, curly, brown hair.

"Good morning Mithter Thunthine," she announced with a big smile.

With that simple welcome she was off and moving. She skipped along the hedge that lined the side of the old two-story yellow house with white, decorative shutters on the sides of each window.

She hesitated before quickly running past an old cellar door that led to a small cement-floor basement, making sure no one was there to grab her ankles beyond the creepy, locked, hinged doors.

She continued to the end of the hedge and turned to the west side of the house where a large picture window faced the yard from the living room. At the corner of the house was a small screened in porch.

Stopping for a brief moment, she envisioned Grandma Rothie—who visited part of the year—sitting on the porch drinking coffee while reading her morning paper.

Two smaller windows were next to the porch. One was in the den where the 'theriouth work' as she put it, was done. The other window was in Grandma Rosie's bedroom.

The south end of the yard was large and full of pine, lilac, blueberry, maple, and oak trees. Its openness provided a wonderful space for her and neighborhood friends to play endless games.

Beyond the yard near the side alley and behind a row of lilac bushes was her mommy's garden mixed with vegetables and flowers. The garden was given constant care to make sure no unwanted weeds grew or bugs resided. This summer it embraced tomatoes, carrots, lettuce, cucumbers, and squash. Around the perimeter of the garden were rows of beautiful, yellow sunflowers. She was amazed how tall they'd grown and wondered if they'd ever one day reach the clouds.

She loved stepping in and out of the rows to see if she could jump higher than their faces. She'd stare, pretending they were dancing fairies wearing flower petal hats around happy smiling faces. At times it seemed like they watched her, asking her to join in their dance. On other days they appeared to taunt and ignore her, turning their faces away towards the sun.

This was when she pretended the flowers were in trouble. "Thunflower? Look at all thith dirt. Didn't I tell you to clean your floor before you tharted danthing? Don't turn away, I know you hear me."

The taller they grew the more curious she became. On sunny days they'd consume her with their beauty, and on cloudy days their drooped petals signified something inside of them had died.

How do they grow so tall? Why are they yellow? My dandelion bracelets are yellow. The sun is yellow. My house is yellow. I have a yellow hair ribbon. If I picked one, would Mommy have a big enough vase to keep it in the house?

To the right of the garden was a swing set equipped with seesaw, monkey bar, ladder, and a swing she pumped so high she could almost touch her toes to the sky. Next to the swing set stood a beautiful old oak tree that spread its branches low, inviting her to one day climb inside.

The east side of the house was lined with tall evergreen trees and hedges. In the summertime the hedges were graced with beautiful, white, hanging lace.

Off the back entrance to the house was a patio with a green steel railing surrounding a concrete platform. The aluminum roof was made of green and white metal shingles. She entertained her imaginary guests on the patio by serving lemonade and cookies her mommy made for her to share. She'd read a fairy tale or share a favorite song. On special occasions, she envisioned her daddy had joined her, and together, they would sing.

She'd just begun picking dandelions in the side yard to make one of her special dandy bracelets when her mommy called from the den window.

"Joy, it's time to come in, honey, and get ready."

She didn't answer at first, curious how the color yellow had appeared on her fingertips. After studying, her inquisitiveness turned to the space between her forefinger and thumb where, after deep thought, she concluded most definitely use to have a finger there.

"Joy, come on in, honey. It's time to go." Her mommy's firmer shout this time indicated time was of the essence.

"Where, Mommy? Where do we have to go?" she replied while collecting dandelions that had fallen from her grasp.

"We're going to the train station, honey."

This definitely got her attention. There was only one reason why they went to the train station. She ran excitedly to the house.

"Grandma Rosie's coming today," her mommy exclaimed.

CHAPTER 3

Every day brought with it a new adventure or so it seemed as a child. Everything became alive as soon as she set her thoughts free.

Grandma Rosie carried a small rose embroidered pillow stuffed with goose feathers, soft and squishy to the touch, on her long train ride from Arizona to Cherry Grove. The pillow fit easily in her suitcase, but she chose to carry it on her lap.

It gave her comfort to touch the soft pillow. Snug underneath her arm, it provided security and protection if ever needed. The pillow traveled with her as a companion, a friend, on the journey. She protected it as much as it protected her.

The train slowed as it approached the next to the last stop before reaching Cherry Grove. She collected her things from the empty seat next to her.

She chatted with a businessman dressed smartly in his suit and tie on his way home from Chicago. He appeared worldly for such a young man. The train ride passed quickly while she listened to him talk about his recent travels.

His adventures came alive while he spoke making her feel she was experiencing those parts of the world herself. "While in Paris, did you see the Eiffel Tower? I've read the iron lattice design is magnificent, especially when viewed up close," Grandma Rosie questioned.

"Oui Ma'am, j'ai vu le Tour Eiffel." He humorously responded with a French accent.

She laughed pretending to understand, but if he asked her to repeat in English she would have said, "Yes Ma'am, I did a tour but fell?"

"You'd be amazed how fast the metro goes. If I were a betting man I'd say it reached speeds of fifty or sixty miles per hour, but when I asked the conductor, who spoke English, I found the average speed was only thirty to forty miles per hour. Did you know the majority of the routes are underground? This train today seems to be puttering along, but hey, gives us more time to chat."

As he spoke on and on, her thoughts drifted. Did he have a family back home? If so, how hard had it been to be away for so long?

"Did I mention the cathedrals? Each one is like a palace, spectacular. The architecture is amazing, the various steeple heights each masked amongst ornate buttresses and pinnacles. You have to wonder how they constructed and engineered such brilliant designs so long ago."

He described in detail the unique differences in agricultures, and how genuine the local people were in the various countries. He described how curious they were of him, staring as he tried to converse in English with local food merchants.

"Most of the time I simply used hand motions and pointed to what I needed. You couldn't miss following these oversized hands of mine now could you?"

She glanced at his large, muscular hands as he went on to describe the size of buildings, length of vineyard rows, and the vast and awesome alpine mountain range.

"I went hiking near the town of Kitzbuhel, Austria, a few miles east of Innsbruck. A grand medieval town, made you feel like you took a giant leap back in time. The view from the mountain range was magnificent, unbelievable beauty— just took your breath away."

She noticed he wasn't wearing a wedding ring.

Hmm, not married.

"I won a hand of Black Jack in Monaco. Did you know it's the second smallest country in the world? It's located at the start of the French Riviera."

"Do you have family young man? Children?" she interrupted with a caring smile.

He sat back in his seat, rested his head against the oversized headrest and slowly closed his eyes. She waited to speak. It was the first quiet moment they'd shared since they began to talk over an hour ago.

He appeared as if he'd entered another country, but this one was not of this world. Maybe he was traveling to a different time in his life, his youthful look slipped away from his face. He opened his eyes.

He seemed content yet lost, as if living a life he hoped would cover the reality he recently experienced.

"I do but...." he said and hesitantly added, "I mean I'm not...."

The loud train whistle sounded while they traveled quickly through a small town she recognized from her youth. The train reduced its speed. Passengers started collecting their belongings. They'd reach their destination soon. She was compelled to continue the conversation, yet time was now limited. She reached inside her travel bag and pulled out a small green embroidered pillow lined with ruffles. She glanced at the pillow for a moment, nodded, and handed it to the young man.

"What's this?" he cautiously asked.

"It's a gift," she replied with an enchanting smile that creased her soft lined cheeks.

"I don't know what to say. Thank you and please know I'm grateful, but I can't accept it. It's such a kind gift but you barely know me."

"Yes, as a new acquaintance that's true, but I've so enjoyed our chat and listening as you shared your adventures. My goodness, it seems you've traveled all over the world. Please, take it."

He carefully held the small gift that resembled an oversized marshmallow in the open palm of his large, callused hand.

"Now, I'd like to share something of my world with you," she continued. "You see, I sense a good character in you though perhaps somewhat troubled. It's as though you're looking for an answer about something or perhaps about someone. Am I right?"

"Well, yes but how could you know—?"

"As I listened to the stories you've shared on our short two-and-a-half hour train ride, there was something I found missing behind those tired and drawn blue eyes. Did you realize you never mentioned another living soul, not one? Forgive me, but I must ask a question."

His soft gaze turned into a guarded glare as if he knew what she was about to ask. It wasn't her intention to put him on the witness stand, but she couldn't stop the impulse to move forward.

"Was it by chance you traveled to all those countries alone, or did you travel because you simply wanted to be alone? Or, if you were totally honest with yourself, is it because you wanted to be left alone?"

She sat back in her seat and waited while the young man's face turned pale as though his mask had been uncovered. His disguise seemed dark, troubled, not ready to be revealed to anyone, most of all himself.

"You don't have to answer, dearie." She sent an assuring smile. Maybe he was trying to distance himself from her as he became vulnerable to his own truth.

"Please, I want you to have the pillow. You see, I've always loved to collect pillows. It's a hobby of mine I've enjoyed for years starting back when my husband Charles gave me...." She caught herself before her thoughts trailed off to another time.

"Well, let's just say I've collected them for a long time. I share the pillows with people I think will appreciate them. You seem to be one of those special people." Her eyes moistened behind her wire framed bifocals.

His tall slim body rose in front of her. He glanced down, stopping himself from a natural impulse as though he wanted to give her a hug, but instead held out his hand.

She reached up with both hands, took his and gazed in his eyes. "Now that you're home, take time to go for a long walk. Don't look down, look up. See the beautiful scenery around you. Ride your bike out into the country. Take deep breaths, smell the air. Catch a flock of geese flying overhead. Note their formation, at times it's perfect, just as you and I try to be. At other times their formation is awry or bowed yet, they still arrive to their destination safely, don't they? Listen. There are whispers in your heart. They speak to you, but you have to listen closely. Do these things, young man, and I promise, you will begin to find the inner peace I sense you're seeking."

The familiar whistle blew as the train came to a complete stop. The young man nodded with a soft smile, slowly pulled his hand away and walked down the aisle to exit the train.

Still feeling the warmth of his hand, she leaned down and picked up her purse and bag, tucked her own pillow under her arm and started down the aisle. She glanced out the train window and recognized two radiant faces. One wore a loving, caring, and familiar smile that reflected an abundance of warmth and affection—Emmy. The second was unable to contain herself while she bounced up and down trying to find her—Joy.

The train conductor took her arm when she approached the stairs and helped her down the platform where her daughter and granddaughter eagerly awaited.

Beyond their faces off in the distance she recognized the young man whom she had befriended. He had stopped for a moment and was staring down at the pillow; the gift she had freely given. She watched him while he read the pillow's inscription.

Listen to your heart for it will always lead you home.

She prayed it would help him find his way.

Emmy and Joy ran to her. She embraced them and held them tightly.

For a while, she was home.

CHAPTER 4

Make way for the sandman. Rock-a-bye and good night.

Even for a five-year-old, Joy was very observant of her Grandma's appearance. Grandma Rothie always wore a hair net. Sometimes it was worn over small steel curlers coiling her black dusted gray hair. The curlers resembled the kind used when she got a perm.

Grandma wore beige moccasins that slipped on easily. Each slipper had a tie on the top that held small varied color beads. The bottoms were worn and when she strolled down the hall from her bedroom they created a soft scuff noise against the old wood floor.

She wore clear nylon stockings, one on each leg, neatly rolled down from the top of her thigh to just below her knee cap. The nylons barely masked the bulging veins at her ankles. Her dark blue flowered jersey dress had a matching belt and sweater, always a sweater, with a spare tissue tucked in one of the sleeves. A sparkly glass brooch sat at the neck of her dress.

Her neck sagged with aging skin and the top of her hands were wrinkled. Joy could sit by her for hours and make mountaintops out of the wrinkles that disappeared in seconds when she made a tight fist.

Her love was plentiful. Soft blue eyes concealed the strain of years spent toiling on the farm. The small mouth and thin lips hid artificial teeth yet showed a smile of warmth without a word being spoken. Her nose was large which she touched up with powder in an attempt to make it look smaller.

Grandma Rothie had a wart. The growth wasn't ugly nor did it make her cringe, but sat proudly on her face between her thick eyebrows. The wart was a part of her. Like a birthmark to Marilyn Monroe, Grandma's wart defined her.

After Grandma Rothie's arrival, the summer days went by quickly. Joy put herself in charge of programming and Grandma became her first assistant. On sunny days they tended to the garden, picked weeds, and gathered ripened vegetables. One day, trying to help, Joy carried as many tomatoes as she could fit in her outstretched t-shirt trying her best not to drop any. Her challenge was going smoothly until she climbed the stairs to the side porch. One tomato slipped loose. It rolled down the steps followed by another, and another, and another.

By the time Grandma caught up to her, she sat on the sidewalk at the bottom of the steps with smashed tomatoes surrounding her.

She slowly raised her head. "I think I need a bigger thirt," she uttered, defeated.

"That's my girl. Now, let's gather up these tomatoes and bring them inside. Today I'll show you how to make ketchup."

As quickly as the tomatoes fell, her spirit was lifted. Grandma Rothie chuckled, leaned over and kissed her forehead.

The rest of the morning they boiled tomatoes and let them cool. They squeezed them into a large yellow bowl and laughed when the insides of each tomato spurted out between their fingers.

When forced inside by rain days, they built forts, covering the dining room table with blankets from the hall closet. Grandma Rothie was not allowed to enter unless she knew the knock which Joy secretly changed after each visit. They'd play cards including Go Fish, Concentration, War, and Slap Jack which was by far her favorite. She got tickled in anticipation of a Jack appearing at the next flip of a card. Sometimes in her excitement, she'd slap the card before the face could be seen making them break out in laughter.

Their most special time of all was in the morning before Emmy was up getting ready. Joy would quietly creep down the stairs and walk along the hallway to Grandma's bedroom. She could toddle there with her eyes closed by following the scent of lilac from the powder Grandma wore. Her room was always warm and quiet. Old family photos lined the far wall, each in its decorative frame. She had an old maple vanity that supported three large mirrors. Sometimes Joy would sneak by during the day and watch Grandma Rothie take out the small steel hair rollers or adjust her hair to fit inside the mesh.

The furniture in the room consisted of a matching set of maple chasseur drawers, a high double bed covered with a beautiful old family quilt, and a light brown sofa bed positioned along the wall underneath the old photos. Large, small, and decorative pillows were stacked around. Some had cross-stitched sayings and bright colors, others were soft. There was even a plain white one. A few had the name of cities and states Grandma had visited; others were decorated with animals, flowers, dragonflies, ladybugs, and butterflies. Among the large collection were two of Joy's favorites. One was old and worn with a light pink silk case and thin white lace woven around the edges. Writing was stitched in dark purple forming the name— Emma Marie.

25

The second pillow was newer and made of the same light pink silk but a white ruffle was sewn around the edges. It was also stitched in dark purple forming the name—Joy Lou.

She softly knocked on the door and peeked in the room. At times Grandma Rothie looked like she was sound asleep, but if she waited patiently a smile would eventually appear confirming she was pretending. Joy would excitedly respond by quickly running around the bed and hopping beneath the covers.

They'd discuss the day's activities or ingredients for a surprise breakfast created for her mommy before the start of her day. Most of the time they were a team, but on these special mornings the wisdom separating grandmother and granddaughter always became apparent.

She lay quietly in deep thought and stared up at the bare white stucco ceiling. The early morning sun had begun to peek through the small opening between the curtain panels that guarded the picture window above the bed. She knew her prolonged silence would eventually make Grandma Rothie wonder what was bothering her. Her first morning voice came out so softly she wasn't sure Grandma heard her.

"Grandma Rothie? What if...."

"Yes, dearie, go on."

"What if I juth didn't go to thchool thith year?" She never held back her thoughts, and this morning's issue was to be no different. She put it out there plain and simple.

The new school year was starting in a couple of days and as each day drew closer she became more uncertain. She hoped Grandma would see her side.

"Let's think about this for a minute. Hmm, what if your mother didn't send you to school?"

She was relieved with her reply.

"Really, do you think you could talk to her?" She could count on Grandma Rothie. She loved being home, especially when Grandma came to visit.

"Well, you definitely don't need to learn to read, you've been reading for years, at least since you were four."

She nodded in agreement. She picked up reading faster than, as Grandma Rothie would boast—two greased pigs in a hog catching contest.

"You can print your name beautifully, but you'd probably need to have someone write your letters to me when I'm not here. Of course, I'll want to keep up on how you're doing when I'm staying the winters with Aunt Lelia in Arizona."

"Well, yeth," she said with the first hint of uncertainty in her voice.

"I remember your mother's first day of kindergarten and all the other children crowding around wanting to play this game or that activity. Your mother even had to bring an item from home one day for something called show and tell. Do you know they made her stand up in front of all those kids and talk about her favorite toy and why it meant so much to her? Her teacher was always reading stories to the class. Of course, you and I know we can do that right here at home."

Grandma Rothie paused for a moment and glanced down with a sly smile.

"What elthe Grandma Rothie?"

"Every now and then she helped her teacher with the weather board. She'd put up an umbrella sticker if it was raining outside and a sunshine sticker if it was sunny."

"A thicker? A thunthine thicker?" Full attention now turned to Grandma Rothie. She rolled over on her side and marveled at all the exciting things she'd experience in kindergarten.

"She colored and made special art projects. Then, as if she wasn't tired enough, they made her go outside and have recess. She ran around the playground with her friends playing tag, dodge ball, and jump rope. She was always tired when she came home each day. You're absolutely right, honey. I agree, you should stay right here at home with your mother and me."

"Well...." she said hesitantly. She twisted one of her long curls around her fingers in front of her freckled face.

"I thuppothe I could try thchool for a day or two."

"Are you sure? We've plenty to do here to keep you busy."

Grandma Rothie didn't know what she was about to say next would have such a deciding impact on her final decision.

"I bet you could even help us beat the rugs."

If there was one thing Joy detested more than anything, it was beating rugs. One Saturday morning, her mommy had taken their long hallway rug outside and hung it over the clothesline, so it dangled evenly on both sides. Holding a bat, each of them took a side. Her mother gave the count of three. She came out swinging, only pausing to watch dust particles explode and float along the stream of sunlight shining between her and the rug. She wondered if she had created fairy dust since they sparkled.

She wound up for her second attack when she heard her mommy scream in pain. "Mommy, Mommy, what happened?"

"I'll be okay—the wooden bat ricocheted off the rug and hit me in the forehead. Come with me to the house for a minute, honey."

Her mommy quickly grabbed a towel, filled it with ice, and applied it directly to her forehead which was now the size of a small goose egg. They sat down until the pain subsided and swelling had gone down.

Joy followed her every move and direction, overly concerned to see her mommy in such pain. While she rested on the couch, ice on her forehead, she leaned her head softly against her shoulder and cried.

Beating the rugs was a chore she didn't want to ever experience again. Maybe going to school wouldn't be bad after all.

"I think I might try kindergarten, Grandma Rothie. What thould I take for the thow or tell you were talking about? If the teacher athked me if I picked it out, you know what I'll tell her? I'll tell her my very betht friend helped me. Am I your betht friend, Grandma Rothie?" Joy looked up at Grandma for an answer.

"Oh yes, honey, you will always be my life's little Joy." Grandma smiled and snuggled her closer. "I have something special you can keep and take with you to school."

Grandma slowly got out of bed and walked stiffly over to the sofa that held all the different pillows. Joy's eyes lit up. She had always wanted one of her special pillows, the ones she collected and gave to others, to keep for her very own. She perused the pillows and immediately picked the bright yellow one with multi-colored sequins sewn across the top. It'd be her first choice.

Her second was one of the animal pillows. One had two white elephants standing by each other, one with its trunk up and one with its trunk down surrounded by two large green palm trees.

Third choice would be the flower garden pillow. It portrayed a beautiful garden full of red roses, pink daisies, and her favorite, yellow sunflowers.

Grandma picked up one of the pillows. Joy couldn't see which one, but when she turned to walk back towards the bed saw it was the plain white one. No color, no lace, no trim, no sequins, no animals, and definitely no flowers. There was nothing fancy about it. It was stark white.

Her eyes disappointedly followed Grandma as she made her way around the maple bed posts and slowly sat beside her, handing her the pillow. She didn't utter a word, fearful of not sounding grateful.

"This pillow represents you, Joy. I want you to listen to me carefully. I'll try to explain why I chose this pillow for you. I know it's rather plain."

She fidgeted since she couldn't contain herself any longer. She didn't understand. Her disappointment at the moment was evident as she stared at the pillow held gently between her two small hands.

"It'th juth, white," she softly said to herself but loud enough for Grandma to hear.

"But it's yours, Joy. This white pillow represents you as you are right now. Fresh and awaiting all the experiences life has to offer. It is unmarked, pure and clean. I want you to try and keep your own life just as this pillow is now.

"You'll have other pillows in your life, if you choose, that'll represent you as you grow. You'll have pillows with beautiful designs and colors that reflect your life's experiences. I could've given you one of my pillows with a color or a design, but it would have been one that represents my experiences, not yours. Do you see the ruffles around some of my pillows?"

They turned to the pillows with lace ruffles, cloth ruffles, striped ruffles, black ruffles, sheer ruffles, and even polka dotted ruffles positioned on the sofa.

"Pillows that have ruffles represent hurdles I've had to conquer or challenges I've had during my lifetime. I'd love to sit here and tell you that you won't have any, dearie, but unfortunately, they will be part of your life. We all have them from time to time, but what matters is how you get over them or turn the challenges into something positive."

"I had a challenge onth," she said. She got up onto her knees, still holding her new pillow.

"I told my friend, Bobby Thaint Cloud, I could run fathter than he could down our alley between our houtheth and gueth what?"

"What?"

"He thaid okay, but I had to take my thoeth off to do it."

"And did you?"

"I thure did. And I beat him too. He wath tho mad," she exclaimed.

"That you beat him barefooted?"

"No. That I beat him and I'm a girl!"

Together they burst out laughing, and Grandma tried to quiet her down for fear she'd wake Emmy.

"That wath a challenge, right?" She settled down and curled up again next to Grandma folding her tiny arms around her new pillow, hugging it close.

"That's exactly right. We can still hold on to their memory and be reminded of our challenges by making them a decoration in life such as my variety of pillows over there. But what is most important is you face whatever life hands you and move on."

She continued to hold her new pillow tightly and envisioned her first day of school, knowing a pillow with a design or color, preferably yellow, would more than likely be added to her collection soon.

CHAPTER 5

"I love you. I love you too.
You're a good girl. I know it.
S'all right? S'all right!"

Emmy walked to school with Joy on her first day of kindergarten. Joy hopped down the porch steps and continued along the sidewalk pausing for a moment to wave goodbye to Grandma Rosie who stood at the side window blowing kisses.

The school was only four blocks from their house but by the second block, obstacles Emmy considered dangerous, appeared along the route. She needed to discuss these with Joy before she would ever be allowed to walk to school alone.

Children of various ages eagerly made their way to school. There was a group of older girls who giggled and pointed to a group of boys walking ahead. Other children scurried by balancing their steps atop a low cement wall bordering a neighboring yard. A few honked horns when they rushed past on their colorful banana seat bicycles.

"Wow, he rideth that bike fath. Did you thee him jump hith bike up that curb? I'm going to try that thomeday."

She beamed at Joy who gazed up at her, each exchanged smiles.

How did she get this old so fast? Will she really be okay without me? Have I taught her everything she needs to know to be polite, safe, and honest? What if she gets hurt at recess? How did my mother ever do this?

She imagined Joy's silent responses. *I hope she'll be able to let go of my hand, I can barely move my fingers. What will she do all day without me at home? She's pretty much done teaching me everything she knows, it's a good thing I'm old enough to go to school. I'm walking to school alone tomorrow. Well, maybe the next day.*

They approached a busy intersection in front of the school yard. A tall, slender woman with jet black hair pulled back in a bun dressed in a police uniform from head to toe walked out into the intersection with a whistle in her mouth to stop traffic.

"Thanks, Peggy. How was your summer?" Children hailed as they strolled by.

Peggy smiled and greeted each one by their first name. She apparently knew every child that walked within her crosswalk.

They continued across the intersection behind the children. Peggy stood in the middle with arms outstretched until they had passed and then followed until they were safely across the street. When Peggy blew her whistle and waved on traffic, they jumped.

"That'th the loudeth whithle I've ever heard," Joy exclaimed.

She smiled at Peggy and wondered if she might be taken aback by Joy's lisp. People weren't quite sure how to respond without saying something to her first. Peggy handled it beautifully.

"I bet this is your first day of school," Peggy inquired when she bent down to introduce herself.

Joy nodded in agreement as she scouted out Peggy's uniform decorated with buttons, badges, decorative stripes, and a shiny belt buckle. Joy put her hand in front of her eyes to stop the reflective glare from the bright morning sun.

"My name is Peggy and I'm your crosswalk guard. I make sure you get across this busy street safely when you're on your way to and from school. You always wait for my signal; it will tell you when it's safe to walk when you get to the busy corner." Peggy pointed across to the other side of the street. Cars zoomed through the intersection. "Can you be sure to do that for me?"

Joy, again, nodded in agreement.

"Good girl. Now what's your name?"

Joy glanced at her mother and then back at Peggy. The smile had left her face. She knew a more pondering question was about to take place and the too familiar pains of a battlefield coming upon them.

"How many warth have you fought in?" Joy looked again at all the decorations on Peggy's uniform.

Emmy closed her eyes and smiled, shaking her head realizing what Joy must be thinking. As much as she wanted to protect her daughter from the current events in the world, she knew sheltering Joy from their existence wasn't the answer.

She tried to keep a close watch on news stories exposed to her five-year-old. Once in a while, time would get away from her, and she'd find Joy sitting in the living room watching the news broadcast that came on after her favorite afternoon cartoon series.

She'd be busy getting dinner ready and forget to pull Joy's attention away from the television or turn it off completely. Troubles between lands, beyond Joy's comprehension, were changing the world they once knew. She wished she could make it all stop by switching to one of the other three stations. But with every turn of the dial, the proof remained real as the evening news broadcasted the day's events.

She was certain this was where Joy had seen a soldier dressed in uniform and must have assumed everyone in uniform had fought in a war.

Peggy gave a graceful glance to her, smiled and then addressed Joy. "This is a police uniform. I do important duties like make sure people put their nickel in their parking meters. Most importantly, I help little girls on their first day of kindergarten get to school."

"How did you know?" Joy pulled her shoulders back and stood proud smiling at Peggy in amazement.

"Just a lucky guess." Peggy winked. "Now, you better get on your way. You don't want to be late on your first day."

She took Joy's hand and turned to walk to school. Joy stopped for a moment and peeked back towards the intersection. Peggy prepared to help another group of young children cross the busy street.

"Peggy," Joy yelled just before Peggy blew her whistle.

Peggy stopped, let down her whistle, and glanced from a distance at her new little friend.

"My name ith Joy. Joy Miller."

"Nice to meet you, Joy Miller. You have a great day."

As the whistle blew, they strolled along the sidewalk and up the old concrete steps leading to the school building.

Joy's grip tightened as they approached the front door bearing the name, Cherry Grove Elementary School, est. 1928. Neither of them said a word as endless numbers of children arrived from every direction. Younger ones were with parents, grandparents, a sister or brother; older children came to school on their own. Cheerful greetings were exchanged when old classmates saw each other after their long summer vacation.

She held Joy's hand tight, took a deep breath, and glanced down at her. "Ready?"

"Yeth, Mommy, ready."

They walked through the large double doors and entered the school. The smell of old wooden classroom floors and echoes of hard-soled shoes hitting grey and black speckled hallway tiles filled the air. The hallways were busy and introductions from various teachers reverberated. They slowly approached Joy's classroom.

"There she is, honey. That's your teacher, Mrs. Williams."

She glanced down at Joy who tightly squeezed her hand. Joy appeared spellbound as though she were seeing an angel for the first time.

She watched Joy's teacher while she greeted a little boy and his father. She couldn't help overhear the youngster cheerfully telling Mrs. Williams about his summer camping trip and details about catching his first catfish.

They waited patiently until she sent them into the room to find the table with his name. They stepped forward to begin their introduction.

"Welcome to kindergarten. I'm Mrs. Williams. Who do I have the pleasure of meeting?"

Mrs. Williams' voice was soft and gentle, as if she could transition from speaking to song, and no one would know the difference. She had a beautiful smile that welcomed them immediately. Her hair was brown, slightly ratted on top for more height, and flowed down her shoulders ending with a short flip.

She wore a yellow cardigan over a white blouse with a plaid skirt, nylon hose, and black pointed flats. An all too familiar scent of lilac perfume floated in the air around her. A beautiful brooch held her sweater together at the top button below her neck.

She guessed Mrs. Williams couldn't be much older than herself and wondered if she had children. She wiggled Joy's hand which was still in hers and gave her a nudge.

Joy, for the first time in her life, was speechless.

Feeling the necessity to introduce herself, she held out her hand, "Hi, Mrs. Williams, I'm Emmy Miller."

Joy was uneasy and remained guarded, staring at her new teacher. She'd never known her daughter to be bashful and wanted Joy to give a good first impression.

"I bet you're nervous, right?" Mrs. Williams knelt to eye level.

Joy nodded in agreement.

"I was nervous on my first day of kindergarten too. My daddy sat with me for a while in my classroom and told me whenever I felt that uneasy rumbling in my tummy…do you know that feeling?"

Joy quickly nodded up and down.

"Well, he told me I should pretend they were beautiful butterflies of different colors and sizes flying around. Do you like butterflies?" Mrs. Williams asked.

Again, Joy nodded.

"He said the butterflies would stay and keep me company until I wasn't nervous anymore. Pretty soon I got so busy with all there was to do in school, I forgot about being nervous and you know what? My daddy was right. I didn't feel the butterflies anymore. But they stayed with me until everything was all right, and I bet they'll do the same thing for you." Mrs. Williams paused before she asked, "What's your first name?"

Her little girl turned to her as if for reassurance and then looked up at Mrs. Williams.

"Joy."

"Why, that's a beautiful name."

Mrs. Williams noticed a few more children and parents waiting to meet her.

"Joy, why don't you and your mother go inside and look for your name on top of one of the tables. That's where you'll be sitting. I have a few more children to greet, and then I'll be in to see you and begin class."

They strolled into the classroom.

The little boy, who'd been ahead of them in line proudly announced, "Here's my name, Uncle Ken. J-e-s-s-e. Yep, they got it right."

The boy quickly pulled the small chair out from the table letting its legs screech along the tiled floor, plopped himself down, and searched the room for his uncle who was over by the window putting out a cigarette.

Other children were already coloring on sheets of paper Mrs. Williams had left on each table. Some wandered around the room with their parents checking out toys, dress-up clothes, building blocks, and the small kitchen. In the back of the room an arched doorway led to a coat room.

"...but I want to go back home and bake cookies with you," the little girl whimpered as her mother tried to reason with her to stay.

"Here'th my name, Mommy. Look it thayth Joy right here, thath me."

She was relieved Joy had stayed occupied and discovered her name on the table.

Joy glanced over at the little boy who had made such a ruckus earlier and slowly pulled the chair out and quietly sat down, as if showing him this is how it's supposed to be done. She picked up a yellow crayon in the middle of the table and colored.

She noticed some of the other parents had gathered at the back of the room and lined up along the coat room wall.

Since Joy seemed content to continue her coloring, she decided to join them. She gave Joy a quick hug goodbye assuring her she'd stay for a while, and return to pick her up in a couple of hours.

"It'th okay. You can go now, Mommy. My butterflieth are taking care of me."

She blew her a kiss and made her way to the back of the room. She found a small opening towards the end of the line near the coat room exit. She smiled as she walked by the other parents' unfamiliar faces wondering if they would one day be her friends. A spot was open at the end of the line which she squeezed into. She was now next to, of all people, Uncle Ken.

At first there was an uneasy silence. It was obvious they were the only two present who had accompanied their child without a spouse on their first day of school. She was curious as to why Uncle Ken brought his nephew.

Why not his parents or at least one of his parents?

Sure the answer would come in time, she'd need to think of another opening line if she wanted to break the awkward silence.

She avoided his glance and watched the smiling parents, straining to overhear their comments regarding how cute their child was while the children interacted with new classmates. Joy seemed at ease at her table, entertained by fellow classmates, swinging her little legs beneath her.

She was glad she agreed to let her wear her hair in a ponytail with her favorite barrettes, one on each side, and her yellow hair ribbon. As she watched her, she acknowledged how grown up she seemed and how much she looked like her daddy.

You would have been so proud of her today.

She fantasized for a moment Sean stood next to her watching their little girl on her first day of school, certain of his sentimental reaction. He wore his feelings on his shirt sleeves, easy to detect when anything bothered him. He repeatedly brushed down the top of his nose with his fingertips during those times. She silently smiled to herself, envisioning his emotion, but the moment was quickly interrupted when Uncle Ken, without an introduction, leaned close to her ear.

"Did you know we happen to be standing in the perfect location for a quick escape?" he whispered. "Don't you agree this opening kindergarten blah, blah, blah has gotten to be too much? I've got a plan." He leaned closer and touched her shoulder with his hand. "On the count of three, we duck out through that coat room exit just to your left. We can sneak out the side door, bolt down the hall, and be free to start our glorious day. What do you say? 'Bout time the little guys learned to fend on their own, don't you think?"

His breath wreaked of smoke, something she detested. He was dressed in jeans with a sharp crease down the center of each leg, possibly purchased earlier that morning. A plaid red shirt had a package of cigarettes in the front pocket and was tucked inside his jeans secured by a brown leather belt with a large, brass, deer head buckle.

Dirty, old, tan, leather cowboy boots completed his outfit. His thick sandy brown hair, which might have been combed years ago, was cut short around his ears. Whisky bangs hung down to his eyebrows and swerved off to one side.

She chuckled silently. He'd probably been given this new outfit just before he was let out of prison.

How insensitive. I gave no indication I wanted to leave, let alone sneak out of the classroom.

She treasured this experience with her daughter and was shocked he felt compelled and comfortable enough to suggest such a thing. How dare him. He didn't know her.

She quickly regained composure and turned towards him to speak her mind, but he was already talking with someone whom she overheard recognized his nephew. Uncle Ken spoke loud as though he intended for everyone in the room to hear what he had to say.

She couldn't help listening to their conversation and wondered if the couple would be interested in using the escape route Uncle Ken had previously suggested.

What an awful assumption he made. I'm certainly going to give him a piece of my mind. But not in front of a classroom filled with first-day kindergartners. After we leave the room, I'll stop him in the hallway or better yet, outside. Hallways echo.

Mrs. Williams propped the door open with a rubber door stop before she spoke to the parents in the back of the room.

"I want to thank you for your patience this morning while I met with your children. It was wonderful to meet each of you. I'm delighted to be your child's teacher this year and my door is always open if you ever have any questions or concerns. At this time you are free to leave. Please return to the classroom by noon to pick up your child."

Mrs. Williams walked to the front of the classroom to introduce herself again and welcome her students. "Does anyone have a story they'd like to share with the class about their summer vacation?"

She followed the other parents out the door as Mrs. Williams called on Jesse who told the class about a ten-foot shark he caught at his grandpa's lake.

She quickly scurried out of the building in time to see Uncle Ken driving away in a light blue and white DeSoto.

So, he escaped after all. He doesn't know it, but he just dodged a huge bullet.

Suddenly, the moment hit her like a ton of bricks; her precious little girl had started school. The freedom she looked forward to for so long became insignificant and in an instant was replaced with a feeling of emptiness.

She glanced back towards Joy's classroom. As excited as she was to start a new chapter, she was well aware life as they knew it would never be the same. She wished she could freeze the time, but understood the future had other plans.

Let go Emmy, let go. Keep walking.

She turned back, inhaled deeply, and began her short walk home. She kicked leaves and small rocks that crossed her path. She thought of Joy and all the stories she'd have to tell in a few short hours. Mrs. Williams and her immediate connection to her students gave her confidence Joy would have a wonderful year in kindergarten.

She also thought about Uncle Ken. Kenneth? Kenny? Ken. He had a story. What she didn't understand right now is why she cared.

CHAPTER 6

Just sit down and it will go away.

Joy loved school. She came home after her first day telling Mommy and Grandma Rothie all about her new friend, Teresa. Her dog, Tippy, had five puppies. They all stayed inside their house with her family.

"Can I have one, Mommy, please, please, please?"

"No, honey, maybe someday when you're older," Emmy responded. She always stood firm whenever the subject of getting another pet arose.

"My friend Debbie already hath a loothe tooth. Thhe getth a whole dime when the tooth fairy vithiths. Will I get a whole dime? Dimeth might be too heavy, right? Maybe paper money ith lighter to carry. How doeth the tooth fairy know where Debbie liveth?"

"Who else did you meet from your class?" her mommy asked, eager to gear her questions in another direction.

"Any boys?" Grandma Rosie added, chuckling.

"Freddie'th a boy. He'th big, thtrong, and maketh a groovy thling thhot out of a paper clip and rubber band."

"Did she just say, groovy?" Grandma Rosie asked Emmy, continuing her chuckle.

She explained they sat in a circle on a special rug in front of the blackboard and helped Mrs. Williams complete the weather board. She was glad it had been a sunny day outside so another new friend, Debbie, could put up Mither Thunthine.

Recess was fun too. She taught her classmates how to play her neighborhood game of statue. Even her

45

next door neighbor, Bobbie St. Cloud, who was in first grade, came over and helped. After recess, they ate graham crackers and drank milk and laid on special mats for a short rest. It was fun to lay on something new even though it was uncomfortable and cold. Some children brought blankets to lie with, others stuffed animals. She brought her white pillow and snuggled tightly.

They sat at the table and laughed as they chatted and listened to the day's adventures. She topped it off with a big announcement she'd been saving since she got home.

"Gueth what? Our whole clath ith doing a play. It'th called, The Mischievouth Rabbit, and gueth what?" She was ready to burst with her final news. "Gueth whoth the rabbit?" She waited for their response.

"You?" her mommy guessed.

"Nope, gueth again."

She couldn't stand the waiting and quickly blurted out her answer. "Jethee, he ith tho funny. He knowth the anthwer to everything. Anytime Mrth. Williamth athkth a quethtion, Jethee doethn't even raithe hith hand. He juth anthwerth really loud. He maketh everybody laugh. Mrth. Williamth doethn't really want him to anthwer without raithing hith hand. Thometimeth he maketh funny noitheth out hith nothe like thith...."

Loud snorting noises by sucking air in and out of her nose filled the room. She laughed so hard her mommy made her stop for fear she'd hyperventilate.

"He liketh to fith too and he thitth right next to me," she added after getting herself under control.

"Sounds like a real charmer," Grandma Rosie stated, shielding her mouth with her hand. Emmy and Grandma caught each other's glance and smiled.

"Oh, I'm sure he is, just like his Uncle," said her mommy under her breath.

"What part do you get to be in the play, Joy?" asked Grandma Rosie.

"Oh, I have the bethteth part in the whole world. I get to be a real, live thunflower!"

It was as if she'd announced she was going to be Miss Marigold 1968, the local beauty contest held yearly in Cherry Grove.

"I'm going to go out and tell all my thunflowerth right now." Unable to contain her excitement, she jumped up and down. She skipped over, hugged her mommy and gave a tight squeeze to Grandma Rothie.

She started to leave the kitchen by going out the side porch, but stopped and turned. "I juth love thchool," she said with a big grin. With that, she turned and skipped out the door.

~ ~ ~

During September everything seemed to fall into a nice routine. Emmy helped Joy get up and ready for school in the mornings while Grandma Rosie fixed breakfast and cleaned the kitchen, so it was ready for her to begin baking when she returned from walking Joy to school.

She loved to bake as much as Joy loved going to school, creating special and unique desserts and pastries. She packaged each one carefully and marketed her products by selling to social clubs, local bakeries, restaurants, and grocery stores. Grandma Rosie was eager to help when needed.

She especially enjoyed taste-testing opportunities and always gave her honest opinion. Her favorite creations included cream puffs, date bars, almond muffins, a meringue cake torte, and a pineapple coconut cake. If she had time during the weekend, she allowed Joy to help by sifting flour. Joy tried her best to hold the beaters steady while the creamy creations turned white and fluffy. When completely finished, Joy licked one of the beaters and, if she wasn't watching, ran her finger across the bowl.

Brushing aside her bangs, she finished creating a special batch of coconut apricot balls. They needed to be delivered to the local country club for a women's bridge group luncheon before noon.

She thought she'd pick Joy up at school and drop off the order. She was in the kitchen getting boxes ready when the telephone rang. She hoped it was someone with another pastry order, so she quickly ran to the dining room to answer.

"Emmy Miller's Decadent Desserts, may I help you?"

"Mrs. Miller?"

It was a woman's voice that sounded familiar, but she couldn't quite place.

"Yes, this is Emmy Miller."

"This is Principal Bauer, Cherry Grove Elementary School."

Her heart stopped immediately fearing the worse. Her mouth went dry while she waited for Principal Bauer to continue.

"First of all, Joy is fine."

She let out a sigh of relief.

"But we've had a situation occur in her classroom, and we think it'd be best if you stopped by the office before you pick her up from school today. Would this morning at eleven work for you?"

No, I want to come now. She wanted to jump through the phone and talk to the principal immediately. *A situation? Who, Joy? She's just in kindergarten for goodness sakes. She loves school.*

"Yes, that's fine. But...."

Before she asked the obvious questions that pierced her mind, Principal Bauer replied, "Good. Mrs. Williams and I will see you at eleven. Thank you."

There was a click on the other end of the line signaling she had hung up. She set down the receiver and checked the clock on the dining room buffet. It was only nine thirty. She decided she couldn't do anything about it until she knew more about the situation. What she did know was Joy was fine and after all, that was what mattered.

But, why the urgency to meet?

She sauntered into the kitchen and tried to concentrate on arranging the coconut apricot balls in straight rows in the specially designed boxes displayed with her personal label. She'd drive them to the Cherry Grove Country Club before her meeting at the school. It wouldn't take more than twenty minutes. She didn't want the pastries to sit in the hot car too long.

She carefully stacked each of the boxes and grabbed her purse from the hutch in the hallway where she caught a glimpse of herself in the mirror. Her hair was askew. She wore a mixture of flour and coconut sprinkles on her forehead and down her right arm.

She groomed, brushing ingredients off her body. A sweet whiff brought to mind a fancy umbrella drink you'd sip while on a sandy beach. The aroma from pineapple, orange, and lemon juices used in rolling the apricot balls to perfection wafted up her nostrils. In a hurried fluster, she checked herself again in the mirror.

Emmy, you can handle this. Simply shower, change, and go.

She often played a game with Joy, pretending to count the seconds it took Joy after she was sent to get ready for bed. In reality, she'd stop the count as soon as Joy was out of earshot and picked up the count again when her little feet came running down the stairs. Joy prided herself on how fast she could get herself ready. Taking some of her own medicine couldn't hurt and was ready to go again in no time flat.

Slow down, you still have plenty of time before the meeting at school.

She called out to her mother who was doing laundry in the basement and singing along to the music playing from her favorite radio station.

"I'm leaving for a while to deliver the apricot ball order over to the country club. I'll be back after I pick up Joy from school."

There was no reason to alarm her with the call from Mrs. Bauer at this point. Without knowing what it was about, all she'd do was worry.

Like mother, like daughter.

"All right, drive safe, dearie," she acknowledged by yelling back.

She drove to the outskirts of town where the eighteenth century clubhouse was located. A plush green golf course stretched around a tranquil lake nestled amongst rolling hills. Before Sean died, she enjoyed the drive to the club, especially when she made a breakfast delivery.

The early morning ride had always been peaceful. Rabbits hopped along the roadside trail and deer fed on grain in distant cornfields.

For the past five years, now all she pictured was Sean driving on that fateful night. The serenity had vanished along with her peaceful memories, no longer able to envision a passive reality from long ago.

She definitely couldn't let them in now. How she wished Sean was with her. He always remained calm. He knew exactly what to say, how to deal with any given situation. He was the rock that kept her planted.

Why couldn't he have waited to go out that terrible rainy night? Why didn't he wake me? I never got to say goodbye.

For now, she needed to stay focused on dropping off her delivery and getting to school in time to meet with Principal Bauer. When she approached the drop-off circle in front of the club, she was relieved to see Chris, now the club manager, helping an elderly gentleman unload a heavy golf bag.

Chris and Sean had been close friends. After Sean's accident, Chris and his wife, Mindy, took it upon themselves to help whenever she needed anything. Mindy was always there for moral support while Chris sat with her for endless hours helping her understand their finances, a monthly task Sean had handled. After months of finalizing bills, transferring accounts, and closing out Sean's estate, it became clearer what she could afford. Holding on to the house, their first home, was her main priority. Her own determination, along with monies she inherited from the sale of her family's farm, and Chris' financial knowledge, made that possible.

He also developed, operated, and raised funds to install the CGCC's new course drainage system, a state of the art structure recently dedicated to the memory of Sean Rodger Miller.

He waved as she got out of her car to unload boxes. "Hang on Emmy, let me help you with those."

"Thanks, Chris. You don't know how much I appreciate your help. Sorry, I'm in a rush this morning and can't stop to catch up, but I'd love for you and Mindy to come for dinner soon. I'll give Mindy a call next week to set the date."

"Sounds great, Emmy, we'd love to and look forward to seeing you all. Bet Joy's grown a whole foot since we last saw her."

"She'll love seeing you, too and yes, I think she's growing up right before my eyes. She just started kindergarten. We'll have so much to catch up on, Chris. I trust the ladies will enjoy the apricot balls, made them extra sweet." She carefully handed the stack of boxes to Chris.

"That's good. As you know, those ladies need some sweetening. Have a good one, Emmy. We'll see you soon. We'll bring the wine."

She slipped back into her car with an uneasy feeling of nostalgia. Seeing Chris always brought back memories of Sean which flooded her senses. Although the recollections were happy ones, she was always left with a familiar sense of emptiness before they slowly dissipated from her mind.

Focus Emmy.

Before leaving the circle drive, she quickly grabbed an eyebrow pencil from her purse and wrote a note on a scratch piece of paper reminding her to call Mindy. She quickly made her way to the school.

When she arrived, a group of young children were involved in a game on the playground, and she wondered if it was Joy's class. She searched the faces.

She pulled her car into a parking space along the side of the road.

Focusing on a short blond-haired boy with black framed glasses, she recognized their neighbor, Bobby St. Cloud, which confirmed it was a first-grade class.

After climbing out of her car, she threw her purse over her shoulder and strolled up the long concrete sidewalk to the school. Her heart pounded with each step to the entrance of the building, as though she were the one in trouble.

She couldn't remember a time growing up when she had been sent to the principal's office, always the good kid who never created conflicts or brought attention to herself. Joy was like her that way. Whatever this meeting was about, she would address it quickly. She entered the building and climbed the wide set of stairs leading to the second floor office. Reaching the top, she glared ahead at the glass door with the imprinted title, *Principal's Office*. Before entering, she reassured herself everything was going to work out fine.

Her hand shook as she slowly turned the knob and entered. A young secretary with black hair and a bright welcoming smile greeted her when she approached the front counter.

"May I help you?"

"Yes, I'm Emmy Miller. I have an appointment to see Principal Bauer at eleven."

She followed the secretary's eyes which glanced at the clock mounted high on the wall above the principal's door. It was three minutes after eleven. The secretary's once welcoming face turned faintly disapproving.

Do I really need to give an explanation as to why I'm a few minutes late?

Before the secretary replied, Principal Bauer opened her office door.

"Mrs. Miller?" The principal firmly extended her hand.

"Yes, it's a pleasure to meet you." It was like she was shaking an old rusty pogo stick instead of a hand. It was anything but warm.

"The pleasure's mine. Please, come this way."

She followed her giving one last glance to the office secretary who displayed half a grin. It was obvious she already knew her fate. Mrs. Williams stood up to greet her. Everything so far was cordial. She waited cautiously for the other shoe to fall.

Principal Bauer slowly maneuvered herself behind the large oak desk. Fairly heavy set, she appeared to be in her late fifties. The purple paisley dress with its beautiful lace collar hung down wide from her neck to below her knees.

This must be the true meaning of the phrase—tent dress.

Black square-heeled, close-toed leather shoes reminded her of correctional shoes advertised in a Montgomery Ward Magazine when she was a teenager in the early 1950's.

Standing behind her desk, Principal Bauer gave the motion to sit. The scenario reminded her of a puppet in an old burlesque show that had no idea or control of where the plot would lead. Mrs. Williams gave her a quick reassuring smile. She waited for Principal Bauer to begin her interrogation.

~ ~ ~

She explained to her mother later that afternoon what happened at school and together decided it would be best if she talked with Joy alone.

That evening after dinner, while Grandma Rosie cleaned the kitchen, she asked Joy to come and sit with her in the living room.

"Is thith a family meeting like you uthe to have when you were growing up?" Joy asked as she skipped into the living room and crawled up on her lap.

"How do you know about our family meetings?" she quizzed, tightening her daughter's ponytail and straightening her yellow hair ribbon.

She remembered the meetings all too well, calling her family a 'three family', because it was Mom, Dad, and she. When one of her parents announced there was a family meeting, it either meant something fun was about to happen or a problem needed to be discussed. She wondered all afternoon how she would begin the conversation with Joy. Explaining a family meeting provided a wonderful introduction.

"Grandma Rothie told me about the meetingth. Thhe thaid one time you got to go to the fair. Are we going to the fair?"

"No, honey. The fair isn't until the end of the summer. We'll plan to go next summer" she replied, not wanting to burst her daughter's bubble.

Joy smiled and snuggled closer into her lap. She held her tight and for a moment they sat in blissful silence. Feeling anxious regarding what she needed to discuss with Joy, she broke the silence with questions that could no longer be averted.

"Joy, is there anything that happened at school today you need to talk to me about?" She waited, hoping for the correct response.

"No," Joy confidently replied after she twirled a soft curl around her small finger for a few seconds.

She closed her eyes in disappointment. She'd opened the door giving Joy the opportunity to explain what transpired on her own. She had declined.

"Are you sure, honey?"

Joy sat upright, turned around, and looked her directly in the eyes. "You mean about the white butterfly I thaw at retheth? It wath tho pretty, Mommy, and it followed me for a long, long time all around the playground and everywhere I went." Joy turned back around and returned to her snuggle position.

"No, did anything happen before recess?"

She was prompting, but wanted to hear Joy's version of what happened. She didn't want to rely on Mrs. Bauer's rendition which might have been a bit one sided.

"Let me think for a minute. Before retheth we colored, did the table work Mrth. Williamth gave uth to do, heard a thtory after thircle time. It wath funny about a porcupine that wanted to thnuggle...."

She stopped Joy's story short, turned her around on her lap and faced her. Joy's eyes indicated innocent confusion.

"What ith it, Mommy? What happened at my thchool today?"

She recognized love and concern in her daughter's eyes. Had the story explained to her earlier really happened?

She used a more direct tactic. "Did anything happen between you and Jesse today?"

"Oh that," Joy continued calmly. "Jethe made me feel bad when we were playing in the kitchen. I wanted to be the cook and he thaid I couldn't. He thaid he wath the one in charge and I had to do what he told me. He wanted me to thet the table and do the ditheth and thath it."

Joy paused and looked up at her. "I wath pretending to be you, Mommy. I juth wanted to cook detherth for everyone." Joy's attention focused on her lap where she had placed her firmly gripped hands.

"What did you do after Jesse told you to clean the table and do the dishes?"

"I walked right over to him, looked him in the eyeth and thaid, no Jethe, I'm cooking detherth." Joy stopped and sadly looked up. "Am I in trouble for yelling?"

"That depends on what you tell me next. What happened after you told Jesse no?" She prayed Joy would simply tell her the truth.

"He thaid I didn't know how to talk right and told me I couldn't play in the kitchen anymore if I didn't do what he thaid. I told him I talked juth fine and if I wanted to cook in the kitchen I would!" Joy took a deep breath. "I felt like beating a rug right then, Mommy." Her face was red and she glared at her.

"Did you?" she asked, not wanting to hear her answer.

"Did I what?" replied Joy, confused by the question.

"Joy, did you hit Jesse?"

The piercing crash of an aluminum pan hitting the bare tiled floor exploded from the nearby kitchen startling them. They leaned to see Grandma Rosie bent over to pick up the pan she'd been drying and she hurriedly returned to work by the kitchen sink. She suspected Grandma Rosie had been listening by the doorway.

"No, I didn't." Joy slowly looked back at her with half a grin. "But Freddie thure did." Her smile grew bigger.

"Freddie?" she responded loudly and confused. "Freddie hit Jesse? Are you sure?"

Pleased it wasn't Joy, she couldn't believe how the story had been twisted when explained to Mrs. Williams and Mrs. Bauer.

She was proud Joy had stood up to him instead of backing down, which she most likely would have done at that age.

According to Joy, Freddie, in his oversized confidence, overheard the argument and Jesse's bossing long enough and took it upon himself to put Jesse in his place.

"Freddie said he got him right in the gullet. What's a gullet?" Joy added giggling. "When Mrth. Williamth came over and thaw Jethe crying, Freddie and I had left to play inthide the block houthe that Jo Ellen and Debbie built. We were their thpethial guethth."

"Do you know what finally happened to Jesse?"

"I don't know," Joy responded, shrugging her shoulders.

"Jo Ellen'th mommy came to help in the clathroom and I thaw Jethe leave with Mrth. Williamth, but he didn't come back until we went to retheth. I bet Freddie punched him tho hard he got thick."

Joy had said all she could to help her understand. To her daughter the situation was over and done with the moment after it happened. She sensed Joy never gave the situation another thought and probably wondered why she'd asked her to explain about it in the first place.

"Can I go help Grandma Rothie in the kitchen before thhe dropth another pan? I need to let her know my pillow ith thtill white."

She nodded, gave her a tight squeeze and helped her slide off her lap. Before skipping to the kitchen, Joy turned to her and said, "That wath our firth family meeting, right?"

"Yes, honey it certainly was. Tight hugs, sweetheart." She returned her smile.

"Tighter oneth back, Mommy," Joy replied distantly while she skipped into the next room in route to Grandma.

She sat in her chair and wondered whether she should phone Mrs. Williams tonight or wait until morning. She felt bad but proud of Freddie. Although she didn't condone hitting, he did what he thought was right. She couldn't fault him for stepping in and sticking up for her daughter who she feared in time may have done exactly the same thing.

One of her main concerns when Joy started school was the possibility of teasing. She scheduled speech sessions twice a week hoping to speed up her progress which she had already begun to see.

It's probably more my problem than my daughter's anyway. She smiled to herself.

Then there was Jesse. Hopefully, Mrs. Williams would handle the situation tomorrow once she was aware of what transpired and call his Uncle Ken and relay the story so he could talk to Jesse. If not, she'd have to take matters into her own hands.

That would be strike two for dear old Uncle Ken.

She crawled into her empty four poster double bed that evening and sank beneath the down comforter and fresh linen sheets that warmed her cool bare legs beneath her gown. Laying back on her pillow, she closed her eyes and slowly let thoughts of Sean enter.

She missed him immensely, and her heart ached deep within.

The past five years had helped to lessen her tragic loss, but fresh, vibrant memories could almost be touched. She envisioned his beautiful smile when he woke next to her each morning and sensed his strong, masculine touch. She envisioned his face—deep blue eyes, soft dimples, and long rough chin line.

His hair was like Joy's, sandy brown and curly when it grew long. He'd do that for her. He knew she loved running her fingers through the curls lifting them from his scalp and watching them shoot down after her fingers set them free.

Sean kept his hair short in the summer since he was outside most of the day. It was a necessity since the temperatures commonly rose into the nineties with high humidity. Sean and his staff worked in scorching conditions quite common to Midwest summers.

She'd often make the drive to the club and meet him for dinner at the end of his day. On a cool summer evening they'd sit outside on the veranda overlooking the eighteenth green, sipping wine, sharing dreams, and watching their private sunsets.

Tonight she lay in the stillness of her room and let her thoughts drift back to another time. They met in high school. He was on the basketball team. She was his biggest fan cheering on the crowds of students and fans in the 1956 regional championship. Her continuous gallop along the sidelines of each game got everyone involved while they watched Sean and the rest of his teammates make one basket after another bringing a solid victory.

Their senior year she received her nickname from the team which lasted throughout their married years—

Flutterby. Flutterby? She opened her teary eyes and sat up in bed, remembering something Joy said earlier that evening.

"You mean about the white butterfly I thaw at retheth? It wath tho pretty Mommy and it followed me for a long, long time all around the playground."

Butterfly. White butterfly?

She reached past her nightstand, pulled out a large encyclopedia from the oversized bookcase that spread along the wall beneath her bedroom window, and plopped the heavy book on the bed next to her.

"B...butter...butterflies...white...here it is," she said out loud.

When she read along the page, gently guided by her finger, she couldn't stop her already-filled weepy eyes.

White butterflies symbolize passed spirits that continually seek to protect you.

She closed the heavy book and placed it on the floor near her bed and slowly laid down. "I wonder. I can't help but wonder."

She drifted off to sleep and dreamt about Joy running freely in a grassy field surrounded by rows and rows of her favorite tall, yellow sunflowers. She could barely spot the soft brown curls on the top of her head as she ran and jumped between the straight and narrow rows. Whimsically following Joy as she ran amongst her beauties was an elegant, white-winged butterfly.

For the first time in a long time, even in her dreams, she was at peace.

CHAPTER 7

Kindness is the highest form of intelligence.

Emmy hung up the phone after her conversation with Mrs. Williams. A weight had been lifted off her shoulders after confirming Mrs. Williams had cleared up the situation with Principal Bauer and Freddie's mother earlier that morning.

She hoped Freddie's mother would go easy on him even though she agreed he had a lesson to learn about picking fights, especially at school. Still, she wanted to thank him for his courage in standing up for her daughter when he sensed she needed protection. Not every five-year-old would have that kind of courage.

She made a mental note to seek out his mother during their performance of *The Mischievous Rabbit* scheduled for the end of the week. She wondered why Mrs. Williams hadn't mentioned Uncle Ken and, quite frankly, was afraid to ask what his reaction had been. Had he been shocked when he heard the news about his nephew and realized someone had gotten the better of him?

She had bad thoughts toward Uncle Ken and wondered why she was so overly annoyed whenever his name came up. She admitted she hadn't been totally fair or given him a chance to explain his desire to escape on that first day of kindergarten. Maybe he was only escaping and had simply asked her to be a decoy? Or maybe he wasn't Jesse's uncle at all? It didn't matter one way or the other.

She did want to chat with him about Jesse, preferably in person, and knew whenever that time came she'd approach the conversation with kindness and an open mind. They'd gotten off on the wrong foot. He was probably a nice person deep down, underneath his tangled hair, worn out cowboy boots, and bulging belt buckle bigger than a bread basket.

Stop Emmy.

She sat at the telephone bench in the dining room across from the long built-in buffet along the east wall. The bench was made of maple and had a soft rose cushioned seat and attached backrest. A round pink princess phone, with a clear rotating dial, sat atop the stand.

Beneath, on the lower shelf, was the telephone book which she pulled out and found the class directory she had placed inside. Mrs. Williams had given the listing to each parent on the first day of school. She located Jesse's last name Hancock and thumbed through the alphabetical pages. She searched the first names for Ken or Kenneth, but to her surprise none were found.

"Maybe he lives out of town and was visiting. Hmm, wouldn't that be a shame," she uttered out loud sarcastically.

Due to the rare silence in her home, the ticking clock on the mantel across the room caught her attention. She was pleased her mother got out of the house this morning to shop with her good friend, Gert. Her mother loved shopping, and it allowed her precious time on her own. She was always full of new stories and bargains to reveal when she returned.

Startled by the telephone ringing next to her, she threw up her arms sending the telephone book flying off her lap and halfway across the room. Shaken by the noise, it took her a moment to pull herself together and answer. As always, she hoped it was a new customer.

"Emmy Miller's Decadent Desserts, may I help you?"

She waited for an answer, but there was no immediate response.

"Emmy Miller's Decadent Desserts. Hello? Is anyone there?"

Another short pause, then a man's familiar voice spoke.

"Did you actually say decadent as in, um, decadent?"

She couldn't believe his timing. *Open mind, open mind*, she quickly reminded herself.

"Yes, I did. May I ask who's calling?" as if she didn't already know. Her guard was up and this time, if needed, she was ready and waiting to speak her mind.

"I bet your desserts really are decadent. I just haven't ever heard any desserts described as decadent before. Small town living I guess. I like that word, decadent. Kind of reminds me of a dessert and toothpaste all wrapped into one."

His exuberant laugh was so loud she pictured him lying on his back, arms and legs in the air as if he wanted to be calmed by someone rubbing his belly.

Her first impression was reconfirmed—she despised him. How arrogant. He didn't even give a simple introduction. Did he assume she knew it was him? Well, she did, but he should still introduce himself. She'd already heard enough and was ready to hang up when he spoke again, this time in a softer tone.

"I'm sorry, forgive me, maybe I'm being rude. This is Ken Kavanaugh, Jesse Hancock's uncle from school. I was told what happened between your daughter and

Jesse yesterday. I'm sorry she misunderstood him. I wanted to call and let you know we've spoken to Jesse, and he promises to be more sensitive to her situation next time. It shouldn't happen again."

Frosted chills rushed through her body. Her anger grew like a volcano inside ready to erupt. What was he talking about? Obviously, they'd heard two different renditions of what happened, Jesse's version and the truth. Joy misunderstood Jesse? He'll be more sensitive to her situation? Her head swarmed with fever. She searched deep within to create a civil reply.

"I know it's probably none of my business, but I do know a great doctor near Cherry Grove that could help your daughter with her speech problem," Ken added.

His final statement pushed her over the top and for a moment speaking civil became the furthest thing from her mind. She held the phone out from her ear allowing a breath to emerge from deep beneath her ribs, calming nerves he had so thoroughly shaken. She couldn't keep an open mind when it came to Uncle Ken Kavanaugh. She was angry—angry at someone she barely knew.

Then, as if Sean had come into the room and whispered in her ear, she remembered a saying he always used that helped when he had a disagreement with an employee at work.

Kindness is the highest form of intelligence.

Her mother had stitched it on a pillow and gave it to Sean the Christmas before he died. The pillow still sat on the top of the bookcase in her bedroom. Repeating the saying over in her mind surprisingly helped her reply with an answer she didn't expect.

"Mr. Kavanaugh...." She closed her eyes as she proceeded to force out the next sentence. "Could you meet for coffee to discuss the situation further? Perhaps soon, maybe sometime this week after I drop off my daughter at school?"

She wanted to portray intelligence but it was a high price to be kind. There was an uneasy silence while she waited for his response. He coughed, not the cough when you have a cold, but an awkward cough when you're uncertain how or what to say next. The silence made her anxious. Her heart pounded from stilled anger.

Finally, the silence was broken. "Yes, breakfast would be nice," he softly replied, his response almost human. "But I'm sorry, I can't this week. Duty calls I'm afraid. I just can't get away," he added.

She surprisingly was disappointed by his reply. She wanted the chance to explain Joy's actions and was willing to hear Jesse's side. She didn't want to delay the meeting too long, afraid it would only make the situation more awkward down the road.

"Are you still there? Hey listen, I'll have my sister give you a call regarding Jesse. Maybe she can meet with you some evening since she works during the day. Of course, the simplest thing would be to stop by and talk to her at school."

She remained quiet while she tried to figure out if she actually knew his sister and put together the pieces of his family. Ken was Jesse's uncle and assumed he was his legal guardian since he was the only adult she'd ever seen with Jesse. Hopefully, Jesse had participating parents.

"Of course," she replied as though she knew who his sister was all along. "How can I reach her at school? Maybe, um, perhaps I'll call the office?"

Why had she stuttered? She was chatting with Uncle Ken, not Principal Bauer. Ken Kavanaugh—she really liked the sound of his name.

He laughed heartily. It probably occurred to him by her awkward answer and questions she had no idea who his sister was let alone where she worked.

"Well, this is a good one. You didn't think *I* was raising Jesse? Oh wait, you did and I apologize. I should have started the conversation by telling you my older sister is Jesse's mother. She teaches right down the hall from the kindergarten class at Cherry Grove Elementary."

Ken gave another deep laugh, so deep he coughed. She pictured him smoking a cigarette and immediately rolled her eyes, thankful he couldn't see her. Still, she had been caught pretending, and he knew it.

"That would have been a thoughtful thing to do, Uncle Ken. Perhaps you didn't think before you spoke. Let's say it wasn't very *decadent* of you?" she firmly answered. She smiled thinking she could be funny too.

"You got me there, and you're right. It wasn't very decadent of me. I really do like that word, decadent. My sister is the first grade teacher, Cathy Hancock. She usually goes in early and stays late after school. I help her by dropping off and picking up Jesse whenever I can. Exactly what kind of desserts do you make?"

"Perfectly delicious ones if I say so myself. I've seen Mrs. Hancock down the hallway at the beginning of the day welcoming her students. I've heard she's a wonderful teacher—nice smile."

"Yep, that's Cathy, great gal, great sister too. She'd do anything for anybody, anytime. She seemed to know your daughter."

"Joy."

"Joy?" replied Ken, a confused tone in his voice.

"My daughter, her name is Joy." It was time he used Joy's name. She wasn't sure how long he'd be around and involved in his nephew's life. Hopefully, she'd find out more after she spoke with Cathy.

"Yes, Joy, thank you. I do have a problem remembering names, but let me tell you, Emmy Miller's Decadent Desserts, I'm certain are delicious. I never forget how a person makes me feel after I've met them."

Another hearty laugh erupted into her ear. She wondered about Ken Kavanaugh. He seemed easy enough to talk with, but at times simply came across too abrupt, as if he rarely dealt with people face to face.

"Let me give you Cathy's home phone number. You two can discuss the situation, and I'm certain you'll get things worked out." As he wrapped up his end of the conversation, he thankfully came across more sincere.

He had an attractive voice—deep, strong, and confident. She'd have pictured him differently if she hadn't already met him that first day of kindergarten.

"Again, I'm sorry Jesse became Mr. Commando during their playtime. I'll talk to him and remind him to keep that kind of play at home."

"Thank you, Uncle Ken. That would be a good place to start."

Ken gave her Cathy's phone number, and Emmy made certain she allowed time to speak with her that evening. The sooner she could get the situation settled and off her mind, the better.

"Will I see you at the play this Friday? You know Jesse plays the main character. He has a number of lines to remember for a kid his age and is on stage practically the whole time. I've been helping him practice and if I say so myself, he's doing a great job. He's going to be quite the stud of a rabbit. Going to put old Bugsy to shame I'm afraid," Ken proudly boasted.

"Yes, of course I'll be there. Joy mentioned Jesse was the star of the play."

She emphasized the word star so Uncle Ken's ego wouldn't be shattered although it was probably made of steel.

"Joy also said how much she enjoys listening to Jesse's stories in class. Hear he's always making someone laugh while Mrs. Williams is teaching."

She contemplated telling him the whole story which wasn't hers to tell. On second thought, why not be honest? It was time he heard about his star nephew.

"One afternoon Joy came home and told us how Jesse leaned back on his chair and accidentally fell backwards onto the hard wood floor. Thankfully, Jesse was fine. Of course, all the children thought it was hilarious. Did you know he got right back up on his chair and immediately leaned back and fell on the floor again? Joy said he did this so many times Mrs. Williams finally took his chair away and had Jesse sit on the floor next to her while she finished teaching."

She was beginning to lose control over what was appropriate to tell Ken regarding his nephew. It wasn't her place. Certain issues were bound to come out during parent-teacher conferences at the end of the quarter. Mrs. Williams should be the one to discuss with Jesse's mother. But without thinking, she concluded with one final dig.

"Perhaps the doctor you earlier recommended can help him with his balance issue?"

She had gone too far. That was mean. There was an awkward silence. The same kind they experienced when they stood next to each other in line on that first day of kindergarten. She prided herself when she spoke her mind after being pushed too far, but thoroughly disliked when she did it to the point of being impolite. This time she had been rude and she knew it.

Was Ken going to hang up? If so, why did she care? She couldn't let that happen. Oh, where were her manners and Sean's spoken words now?

Emmy, speak what you feel and make it right.

"Uncle Ken, I'm sorry. I was out of line about Jesse. I had no right to tell you that story. I know you're only trying to help and be the best uncle. I think it's wonderful he has someone like you in his life. I'm sure his mother does too. Again, I'm sorry. I really don't know what got into me. I had no right to judge."

Her words were heartfelt. That's all she could give him right now. It was hard to have an argument or disagreement over the telephone.

Sean and she had made a pact early in their relationship. If they ever had a fight, even though rare, they'd always find the time and place to make up in person. She had to keep reminding herself this wasn't Sean. It was Uncle Ken, who knew nothing of their pact, their marriage, their love.

"Actually, you had every right. After what I suggested to do that first day of kindergarten, I should be the one apologizing. I haven't been myself for quite some time and that is no fault of yours. I know I'm not making any sense right now. I find it hard to discuss issues over the phone, you know? It seems too impersonal. Maybe I could explain someday in person, that is, if you'll give a guy like me a chance."

She was relieved and pleased with the true sincerity in his voice. She'd enjoy having a meaningful conversation with a man again. It had been a long time, especially with someone she cared about.

Cared about? Uncle Ken?

She smiled acknowledging stranger things had probably happened. Her tone changed as though there was a stronger connection to their conversation. She was happy they had begun to talk through their differences. Most of which she was certain Uncle Ken was unaware.

"Yes, I'd like to meet someday. That would be nice. Maybe we'll run into each other Friday morning before or after the play and, Uncle Ken?"

"Yes?" Ken quietly answered, his sarcastic nature seemed to have been put aside.

"It's Emmy."

"Emmy?"

"Sorry, but I was afraid when you saw me at school you'd call me the decadent dessert lady."

Both laughed across Mr. Bell's invention. They'd finally begun to find a common ground. It was called honesty.

"Hope to see you Friday, Emmy, and just for the record, it's Ken to you, not Uncle Ken, just Ken."

They laughed simultaneously realizing what she'd been calling him during their phone conversation.

"Okay, see you Friday, Ken."

The phone line went silent. She sat alone in unwanted silence and wondered if his thoughts echoed the same feeling. Surprising, for a passing moment, Friday seemed a long time away.

CHAPTER 8

A hug around the neck and hold on tight.

It was almost dawn when Grandma Rosie, lying warm beneath her covers, noticed a strange hissing noise in her bedroom. The sound lasted a few seconds, stopped, and began again. She lay still unsuccessfully trying to determine the strange sound. Slowly, she opened her left eye as if trying to find a perfect photo through a camera lens. As her vision came into focus, at the foot of her bed was the shape of a little girl with long curly brown hair and a lightly freckled nose wearing a big smile.

"Thsssssssss, thssssssssss. Morning Grandma Rothie, can you hear my thsss's? Mrth. Anderthon thayth I'm getting better."

Mrs. Anderson was the speech teacher who had worked with Joy twice a week in the classroom since school started. Sometimes Joy would correctly say a word with a 's' sound without realizing, which was great progress. Joy was gaining confidence, which was wonderful for her and her mother to see.

"Good morning, sweetheart."

She squinted towards the illuminated cat clock with ticking eyes that moved back and forth on top of her dresser across the darkened room. Without glasses, it was hard to make out the time.

"Are you sure it's morning, honey?" she asked Joy, still groggy.

Joy hopped over to the dresser and stood on her tippy toes to check the cat clock.

"Um, juth a thecond. Okay, the big whithker ith on the two and the little whithker ith on the thix. That meanth it...." Joy calculated her answer. "It'th two after thix. Am I right?" she proudly announced.

She shut her eyes during Joy's assessment of time trying to sneak in a few more seconds of sleep. She'd stayed up too late finishing a suspenseful romance novel that was hard to put down. Today, she knew she'd pay the price.

"Close enough, honey. Come on, hop in."

It was a morning routine for them, one she would sorely miss during the upcoming winter months when she visited her sister in Arizona.

Joy crawled in her double bed, pulled the comforter up and tucked it under her chin. Her granddaughter was rolled up in a little cocoon, safe and warm. She smiled knowing what the day ahead held. She turned and faced Joy. "Do you remember what you're doing today at school, dearie?"

Joy pondered for a minute and gasped. "Oh, today is when I get to be a thunflower!"

The hall light came on and reflected in her bedroom. Emmy peeked around the door frame.

"Good morning you two early birds. What are we talking about already?"

"Sorry, honey. Did we wake you?"

Emmy shook her head as she walked into the room and sat on the side of the bed by her daughter. Joy sat up and gave her mother a tight morning hug, her smile gleamed with excitement.

Loosening her grip Joy leaned back and said excitedly, "I'm a thunflower today, Mommy."

"Is that today?"

Joy smiled and nodded yes. Her anticipation was feverish.

"Are you sure it's today?" her mother teased, knowing she looked forward to it almost as much.

She pictured Joy wearing her precious yellow sunflower outfit and spouting lines along with her classmates. All the students had practiced the last few weeks and the day ahead would hold special memories for everyone.

Out of the blue Joy's previous excitement dwindled, as though she prepared herself for a dramatic announcement. She'd gone from a bubbly child to someone who was about to tell a hundred hungry soldiers they were out of food. They remained silent, waiting for her to speak.

"I have thomething to thay to both of you and ith theriouth."

They exchanged smiles. Something deep within Joy's soul was trying to muster its way out. She sat up on the bed between them and concentrated on what she was about to say.

"Here goth nothin. Today, I'm...going to be...a...." There was a slight pause. Joy glanced at them again. They knew she didn't like leaving circle time twice a week to practice with Mrs. Anderson. She complained it took her away from her friends and Mrs. Williams.

Joy's goal in her speech sessions was to practice more than she ever had, so she could rejoin her class. Mrs. Anderson informed them she was working hard and wanted to overcome her lisp probably more than beating Bobby St. Cloud running barefoot down a rocky alley or building a block tower higher than Jesse Hancock.

They watched. She confidently shaped the sound in her mouth like Mrs. Anderson had taught her.

"S...s...s...s...sunflower!" Finally, she spoke loud and clear.

They dropped their jaws and gazed at Joy in amazement. The room erupted with applause and shouts of congratulations. All three laughed and giggled while they surrounded Joy with tickles, kisses, and hugs.

It was six-twenty in the morning. Today was already a very special day.

~ ~ ~

They walked into the school building later that morning to attend the play. Emmy motioned for Grandma Rosie to go to the gymnasium and save their seats. She wasn't sure if Mrs. Hancock would be free, but she wanted to at least stop by the first grade classroom and introduce herself after the nice conversation they had the previous night on the phone. Cathy had been receptive and understanding about the situation and attributed it to her teaching and early childhood education background.

"Jesse can be a little overbearing at times, I know," Cathy began. She recounted their conversation over the phone. "With both children being an only child, well, I guess it makes them doubly stubborn. To be honest, I give your Joy a lot of credit for standing up for herself. I know that's a heavy task when it comes to Jesse. Believe me, I've been in similar situations with him many times."

She listened intently and imagined how different it would be to raise a son. She pictured Jesse digging up worms, having to mend torn jeans, and the ultimate chore of caring for the various lizards, frogs, and goldfish. The visions made her shiver.

She silently gave Cathy credit even though she didn't fully know her home situation. Ken was her brother. She overheard Jesse talk about his grandpa's lake, but hadn't heard any mention of his father.

"I can't imagine the different challenges you face raising a son. It's nice your brother is around to help when needed and rough things up a bit with Jesse," she carefully responded.

She offered Cathy a window to open up if she chose. It probably wasn't the right time or place. After all, this was their first conversation.

"Yes, Dad and I are glad he's finally home. Ken's a little rough around the edges, but deep down he's good as gold. You couldn't find anyone better. Of course, I may be just a little bit prejudice. He loves Jesse like his own and has been a wonderful influence and huge help. They have a special bond. During the weekends they are almost inseparable. Sometimes I'm not sure if that's good or bad." Cathy laughed.

"Jesse reminds me quite a bit of Ken when we were growing up on the farm. They have the same inquisitiveness and imagination which I'm afraid have gotten them into trouble. They speak their minds without much forethought which sometimes turns people off. Neither means to say the wrong thing. It's just what comes out of their mouths. If they could think a bit more before they spoke...." There was a slight hesitation before Cathy carefully concluded, "I know you may have some reservations before giving Jesse another chance, but if you could get to know him better, if Joy could get to know him better, I think he might surprise you."

After they said goodbye and hung up the phone, she pondered the differences between Cathy and Ken as siblings. Her personality was soft, refined, tender, and understanding while Ken's character remained guarded, rough, and sarcastic. She thought deeper—supposing he was even oddly kindhearted. She definitely witnessed Ken speaking his mind, as Cathy explained, without much forethought. Time would certainly tell where second chances could lead but for now, at least for her, the jury was still out.

She strolled down the school hallway festively covered on both sides with a variety of student drawings and paintings. Some colored handprints were transformed into beautiful turkeys. Others were stick-figured pilgrims and Indians sharing a bountiful dinner of yellow corn and orange pumpkins. One row of art work displayed various large turkeys, hand- drawn and filled with colorful beans.

She found it hard to believe the fall holidays were soon approaching. When she came upon the first grade classroom, Cathy was bent over the drinking fountain. It amused her to see how far she had to stoop in order to reach the spout.

"Hello, Cathy? I was on my way to the kindergarten play but wanted to stop by and quickly introduce myself. I'm...."

"You must be Emmy Miller," Cathy responded with a big smile.

"Why, yes?" she replied, surprised she knew her name.

"After we got off the phone last night Ken described you. He said you had, let me think, brown bobbed hair, crystal blue eyes, and a big beautiful smile. I must say, he was right on the money. I know he wants to meet with you. I saw him earlier walking down the hall with the kindergarten class on their way to the gym. He was the only one *not* waving to my class as they walked by." She laughed.

"He brought Jesse to school again this morning to help me out."

Although embarrassed by Ken's description, she was happy to finally meet Cathy in person. She was as genuine and easy to talk to as she was on the phone.

"I hope you're going to be able to see the play?" she asked, assuming Cathy was headed back to her classroom.

"Absolutely, wild horses couldn't keep me away. I grabbed a drink at the fountain and was heading down. May I walk with you, Emmy?"

"Yes, that would be nice."

A crowd had gathered in the gymnasium. Parents, grandparents, siblings, aunts, uncles, and friends lined up and slowly entered the double doorway to the large room in search of seats. Some chatted, others peered over the top of heads to find an empty seat with a good view. She spotted her mother to the front waving her over.

"Come with me for just a moment before you sit down. I know Ken wants to say hello before the play begins," Cathy said as she leaned closer.

She waved to her mother signaling she'd be there in a minute and followed Cathy. They weaved against the entering crowd to the back of the gymnasium.

She anxiously looked forward to seeing Ken, but wanted to be sure she could join her mother before the start of the play. She would make the conversation brief and quickly make her way to her seat.

Looking towards the back of the room, she spotted Ken. He leaned against the wall, his right leg bent to support his stance. This wasn't the man she met earlier. He was clean shaven, his hair had been trimmed and combed. Now he was well dressed with a dark blue, buttoned down shirt neatly tucked into beige corduroy pants. The shiny loafers he wore instead of dirty cowboy boots completed his trendy outfit. If she knew nothing about this man, she would have guessed he was someone's bored relative who was forced to attend the performance.

He was probably looking for his first chance to escape—just like the first day of kindergarten. But, that didn't appear to be the case now. As Cathy mentioned, Ken had been at the school all morning helping with preparations for the play, assisting Mrs. Williams and most likely keeping his nephew, Jesse, in line.

Deep down he's good as gold.

Her heart skipped a beat. She always trusted her heart, but quietly reminded herself, even after five years, her heart still belonged to Sean. She cautiously approached.

Ken stood up straight when they walked across the room, his smile was radiant.

"Hello, Emmy, nice to officially meet you. I'm Ken, Ken Kavanaugh." His voice was deep and he offered his hand. He spoke as if his sister were invisible.

Her knees shook like an insecure schoolgirl. She returned the smile. His handshake was firm, warm, and welcoming. For a moment, neither let go; her hand became lost within his grip.

"Well, isn't this nice. I'm glad you two have finally met and may I say just in time. The play is about ready to start," Cathy said, clearing her throat. She pointed past them to the front of the room where Mrs. Williams strolled to the microphone.

"I'll see you two later," Cathy whispered, touching her shoulder.

Neither acknowledged her departure.

She giggled nervously. She pulled her hand away from Ken's grasp and attempted to regain her composure.

"Nice to meet you finally, Ken. Cathy says you've been helping here all morning?"

Cathy was in the distance greeting parents who arrived late showing them to the last few empty seats. The gymnasium was packed and in a few minutes the only space available would be at the back of the room where it was standing room only.

"Yes, along with Freddie's mom who was kind enough to help too. She did a great job with the girls, helping get their costumes on and hair fixed just right while I attempted to keep all the little guys in line. One boy is easy to supervise but put two together and somehow they find something to get themselves in trouble over. I'd finally get a couple of them into their costumes only to see three others in the play area pulling toys out of the box. I don't see how Mrs. Williams does it on a daily basis." He rubbed his eyes and added, "I could almost use a nap."

Ken gave one of the hearty laughs she remembered during their phone conversation, but this time the laugh fit his personality and strong physique. She surprisingly found it quite endearing.

"Teachers certainly have a gift we should never take for granted. I'm sure everyone in the class will look adorable," she responded.

The lights dimmed. Mrs. Williams began her introduction.

"Oh, here they go. We better take our seats," she whispered quickly.

When she turned around, she was surprised how full the room had become. She stood on her toes and stretched her neck to locate her mother, but the front row of the gymnasium was completely out of sight.

"Did you come with someone?" Ken whispered.

"Yes, my mother. She's in the front row waiting for me, but I'm afraid I can't get to her now. There are too many people everywhere."

Ken took her elbow and guided her across the back of the room. A warm and welcoming, yet surprising sensation traveled through her. There was space to the right of the spotlight in the back of the center aisle where they could see the class when they walked out.

"This will have to do I'm afraid," he whispered. "Can you see all right?"

"Yes, thanks. Hopefully they'll speak as loud as they do on the playground."

They quietly laughed, eagerly waiting for the play to begin. She was sad her mother had to sit alone and probably wondered what happened to her.

On the other hand, she was glad she'd finally met Ken. After speaking with him in person, he surprised her. He was warm and considerate. She also noticed there was no odor of tobacco or the appearance of a hidden cigarette package. That alone was a big improvement.

"Thank you all for coming," began Mrs. Williams. Her voice was as soft as when they met on the first day of school. The room became quiet. Mrs. Williams continued, "I'd like to introduce the Cherry Grove Elementary School's kindergarten class and their special rendition of *The Mischievous Rabbit.*"

The audience applauded when the kindergarten class filed onto the stage. Each child was dressed in a colorful costume led by a glittering yellow sun followed by hopping brown bunnies with pink noses and white ears; a mixture of vegetables including carrots, corn, celery, and what appeared to be a few messy heads of lettuce. The old farmer, played by Freddie, came out in what must have been his older brother's overalls. Both legs were draped in jean material that fell into clumps around each ankle. He wore old high top tennis shoes and a yellow straw hat.

Jesse strolled onto the stage behind Freddie as The Mischievous Rabbit wearing a furry white bunny suit complete with pink ears, pink nose, and a white cotton-ball tail.

Finally, saving the best for last Emmy reminded herself, entered a wide variety of sunflowers in all shapes and sizes. One of the smaller sunflowers, beaming from ear to ear, searched the crowd. She was afraid Joy wouldn't be able to see her next to the bright spotlight. The beam on Joy's face confirmed she'd spotted her Grandma. She appeared relaxed and confident on the stage as if she already owned the audience.

She looks precious. Do you see her, Sean? Do you see your daughter? She's so much like you, so much like her daddy.

Soft murmurs echoed throughout the room when each family member recognized their child. Jesse looked angelic, which made her laugh knowing it was the farthest thing from the truth. He hopped to the front of the stage as the performance began. She glanced at Ken who beamed.

"Jesse looks adorable, Ken," she whispered and smiled.

She was comforted with the sweet reflection in Ken's eyes while he watched his nephew. Jesse truly did look endearing—finally, a positive and overdue thought on her part. Unexpectedly, Ken's facial expression changed from a proud beaming smile, to a look of concern, soon followed by a stare of disbelief. There were no more murmurs or whispers between family members. She turned her attention away from Ken and glanced around the eerily silent room. Gazing at the stage, she caught up to everyone's shocking realization.

Jesse stood alone to speak his first line, his voice frozen in fear.

Ken slowly walked towards the front of the room. His calculated signal indicated Cathy should stay back when she began to make her way towards her son. It was a mother's natural instinct to go to their child when they faltered.

Mrs. Williams, noticing Cathy's hesitation, took her arm and stood close to her. Uncle Ken had been Jesse's biggest fan when it came to his part in the play, let alone the main character.

The room remained hushed. Ken continued his way up the center aisle. His eyes were intense as though he willed Jesse to remember his lines. The audience watched as this unexpected episode appeared to be part of the play. Ken reached the end of the aisle and squatted. Jesse's eyes finally moved below the lights where he spotted his uncle.

"You can do this buddy. You can do this," Ken smiled, nodded his head, and whispered softly.

Jesse's eyes didn't leave Ken's. Perhaps if Jesse could've moved, he'd have run into his uncle's arms crying to be taken home, away from a feeling he didn't understand. He remained fixated on his uncle's eyes.

She moved down the center aisle beneath the spotlight. The other children fidgeted. Some whispered Jesse's opening lines to him.

"Thay it Jethe, you can thay it." She recognized Joy's encouraging words.

But it was Uncle Ken who Jesse looked to for strength. It was Uncle Ken who gave it to him.

"Okay, buddy, you can do this. We're going to pretend we're at home right now. It's just you and me. We're in the living room just like when we practiced. I want you to watch me and we'll say your lines together. *We* can do this together," Ken whispered, his deep voice clearly heard throughout the gymnasium.

He continued to kneel in front of the stage where Jesse stood alongside the stage's microphone. She observed another side of Ken emerge, a nurturing and caring side. He showed love for someone greater than himself. He wasn't going to let Jesse fail, and Jesse's trust in his uncle was evident.

They began Jesse's lines together. "I'm an ornery rabbit and I have a hunger streak...."

Ken's voice could be heard over Jesse's, but as they continued Ken purposely let his voice become softer as his nephew shone on his own.

"I'm coming to your garden, to get something to eat. I'll hop through very quickly to gather up what's good, and eat it down within my hole just like a rabbit should!"

All the vegetables stepped forward and stood with Jesse. He slowly smiled. Sunflowers swayed. They faced Jo Ellen who proudly played Miss Sunshine. Bunnies hopped in between the sunflowers while Freddie portrayed the old farmer who came forward to proudly spout his lines.

Her eyes were fixed on Ken who slowly backed away and walked down the aisle beneath the spotlight. He had to be thankful and relieved the crisis had been averted. He rejoined her at the back of the room. She smiled when he gave a special wink meant just for her. While she stood next to Ken in the darkness, she was rejuvenated. A new warmth and friendship was growing within her, but her heart cried *not yet* as his strong hand gently took her arm and pivoted her to face him.

"I'd like to take you up on your breakfast invitation but instead make it for dinner? Any chance you're free tonight? I don't mean to be too bold, if you think it's too soon."

She stood speechless. Her heart danced.

"We could talk about Jesse and Joy a bit more and maybe, just maybe you could share a few of your decadent recipes?" Ken whispered.

Her eyes glistened in his reflection beneath the spotlight, barely acknowledging his spoken words. They studied each other's features.

"I think I'd love to," she quietly replied without hesitation.

"You think?" Their eyes remained fixed.

"I mean, yes, I'd love to."

They returned their attention to the play as the end of Freddy Farmer's Hoe Down song was bellowed out. Betty Bunny, portrayed by Debbie, came forward.

"Getting into mischief can be fun for a while, but having a family that loves you allows you to have fun for a lifetime," she said to the Mischievous Rabbit.

Both characters nodded in agreement and hopped back in line to join the kindergarten class for their first scene bows.

She applauded and gazed at Ken.

Maybe there were such things as second chances. To once again have—love for a lifetime.

CHAPTER 9

Listen to your heart, but listen carefully, it whispers.

Grandma Rosie chatted with Joy at the kitchen table later that afternoon and reminisced about the play.

They laughed over their favorite parts especially when Freddie, playing the old farmer, accidentally said Jo Ellen's lines. "No need to wear a frown, my rays are beaming down...aren't beaming...um wait, I'm not the sun."

Frustrated, Freddie added with a whisper, "Jo Ellen that's your line."

"I knooooow Freddie," Jo Ellen replied under her breath. She gritted her little teeth, still smiling ever so politely to the audience.

There was also the moment where all eight sunflowers were supposed to sway to the right. Six did, including Joy, but the two in the middle, spontaneously decided the sway should go left creating a domino effect of wavering sunflowers.

"It made me feel like I wath one of my own thunflowerth in the middle of a windthtorm," Joy giggled.

"Who was the man with the deep voice that echoed through the gymnasium? Jesse's father? He certainly was patient and good with the little fella." Grandma Rosie asked the obvious question everyone in the audience had probably wondered.

"No, Grandma Rothie, that was Jetheth uncle. Good thing he was watching. I don't think Jetheth could hear any of uth telling him hith lines." Joy obviously couldn't wait to tell her the circumstances surrounding Jesse's freeze as she put it.

Emmy quietly walked into the kitchen. She busied herself with mindless tasks, picking up a pad of paper from the counter and moving it to the opposite side of the kitchen.

"Oh, I see, honey," she replied to Joy while she watched her daughter.

"Sounds like he just needed a little nudge in the right direction. He did a wonderful job once he got going."

There was a knock on the back porch. Joy ran to answer.

"Hi, Bobby. Mommy, it's Bobby, can I go outthide and play?" Joy asked excitedly.

Emmy didn't respond. She continued to pick up items around the kitchen that didn't need to be moved.

Grandma Rosie got up from the kitchen table and walked over to the porch.

"My, have you gotten taller this fall, Bobby? The cooler air must be helping you grow."

Bobby stood up straight. Head to head he was only an inch taller than Joy. Even though he was in first grade, he hadn't sprouted size wise and was often mistaken for a kindergartner.

"I got a new pair of tennis shoes today. I want to try them out running down the alley. Come on Joy. Betcha I can beat you this time," he teased.

Joy peeked over at her. Grandma Rosie nodded and smiled which secretly told her to do her best. Joy grinned as they walked out. The screen door slammed.

"We'll see about that Bobby Tht. Cloud. I'm not running barefoot thith time."

They walked through the backyard, past the old garage that badly needed painting and into the rock and pebble filled alley, talking and laughing the entire way.

They were like brother and sister, supporting each other in achievements whether it was swinging higher than the other or running faster down the alley.

Sometimes one would get the better of the other and they ended up in a disagreement, but neither held a grudge for long. They were honest with each other and told exactly what they had on their minds. Maybe it was the age that made their relationship so pure. All she knew is they had a special friendship for two children so young.

She ambled back to the kitchen to find Emmy sitting at the table with her face in her hands, crying. She sensed earlier something was bothering her, but had no idea it was anything that would lead to tears.

"What is it, dear?" She joined her at the table and sat next to her.

She knew her daughter well. She didn't get emotional unless something truly upset her. She'd always been the strong one supporting her after her father's death, and showing true strength during the unthinkable—the tragic passing of her own husband.

"You have to tell me what it is so I can help. What is troubling you, honey?" she asked between sobs.

Emmy raised her head from tear-stained hands and gazed into her eyes. "I'm fine, really, please ignore these silly tears. I'm tired and still need to make coconut apricot balls for another ladies group at the YWCA tomorrow night and...and...."

She once again broke down, this time into her Mother's welcoming arms.

"…and I'm all out of or…or…orange juice."

Tears rolled uncontrollably down Emmy's cheeks and onto Rosie's shoulder leaving a dark blue stain on her flowered jersey knit dress.

"Emmy, something tells me the absence of orange juice isn't what's leading you to tears. Whatever is the matter, honey? Has something happened? Are you sick, dear? Is it something concerning Joy?" She held her daughter close and tight while she cried in her arms.

"Talk to me, Emmy. You're worrying me. Oh, honey, whatever this is we'll make it okay. Look at me. Emma Marie, look at me."

She sat back in the kitchen chair and held her daughter out at arm's length, gazing directly into her swollen, tear-filled eyes. Flashbacks of a little girl who would run to her after she fell off her bike and skinned her knee long ago consumed her. The same girl who didn't understand why she didn't make the cheerleading squad her sophomore year of high school, but followed her advice and worked twice as hard and made the team the following year, and the year after. She knew Emmy believed in her wisdom then. All she had to do was hold her daughter tight and tell her it would all work out, and somehow it always did.

"Come with me and let me wipe those sad eyes. We can go in the living room and have a talk."

"Mom, no. Really I can't. I need to check on Joy. I need to run to the store. I need to make a phone call."

"Joy is fine; she's outside playing with Bobby. I'll run to the store for you later and the phone call can wait."

Emmy faced her as if a child again, letting her dab swollen eyes and blowing into the tissue she held. She took her arm and together walked into the living room and sat on the large brown tweed couch in front of the big picture window.

The view allowed her to watch Joy, Bobby, and several neighborhood friends in the side yard playing. She wondered briefly who won the race down the alley. As usual, it probably didn't matter. Whoever won was forgotten by now. They were engrossed in their favorite neighborhood game of statue; if only life could be that simple. She took Emmy's hands.

"Talk to me. That's all you have to do. Just talk to me."

~ ~ ~

Emmy wished she could curl up on her mother's lap just as she had as a child. She stopped crying. Disappointed in herself, she had let her guard down, even with her mother. She had worked hard physically and emotionally the past five years to become stronger and more independent. She'd built a successful catering business, and had hopes of expanding to larger communities nearby.

There had been a young marketing company interested in promoting some of her desserts during the upcoming holiday season. She was flattered for their interest, but had to be realistic fearing she wouldn't be able to keep up with the volume working alone out of her home. It was an opportunity she'd seriously consider once she had capital to expand.

Above all else, she always put Joy first, raising her to be strong and independent with a solid, Christian faith and good moral values.

She'd allowed Joy and her work to consume her since Sean's death, and in doing so, left many scars buried deep inside. Scars that still needed to be healed. Scars that couldn't be healed until she allowed herself to take emotional steps forward.

"It's simple really, Mom. I should've said no. I need to pick up the phone, make a call and just say no. I made a mistake in saying yes; I'm just not ready. I don't know why I said yes; I don't know," she explained, taking a deep breath. Her voice quavered when she looked to her mother for strength. But all she saw was confusion.

"Emmy, you need to back up. What aren't you ready to do? Who do you have to say no to? Is it a big pastry order? You know I'm always willing to help. I know you want to expand someday but...."

She let go of her mother's hands, and leaned back against the soft cushioned couch. She twisted and untwisted the tissue she'd given her.

Slowly she continued her explanation. "I have to call *him* and say no; I can't join him for dinner tonight. I said I could, but I just can't, Mother, I can't."

She glanced at her mother's spellbound face, willing her to guess the reason for her anxiety. Sudden comprehension flashed like a neon sign across her forehead. *My daughter's been asked on a date and hallelujah she finally said yes!*

Her mother had encouraged her to date a few years ago, but every time she considered or contemplated being out with another man, guilt found its way in. She hoped there would be a sign indicating it was time to move on, to finally let go. But so far, no sign had been seen. No signal had sounded.

"Mom, no, I'm just not ready. I can't, I won't." Tears formed again in her tired eyes.

"You can't what, dearie? Simply go out with a man and have fun? Emmy, honey, it's time, don't you see? Five years has been more than enough time. Sean will always hold a special place in your heart, just as you have held a place there all these years for your father, and I'm certain there's a place for me, for Joy.

"Isn't the heart amazing? It's the home for who we are, what we believe, and who we will always love. How? Because, my dear, the heart is where our soul resides.

"No one can ever take the love of those special people from you, but you can certainly add others to it. The heart provides life through its simple beating, pumping blood through your veins, sending all the love that fills it to the outer portions of your being. You are very fortunate to have found love once. Sean, God rest his beautiful amazing soul, was a wonderful husband and would have been an unbelievable father. It would truly be a gift from God to find that twice. Don't let the possibility pass you by because you're holding on to a memory that contains love, but can't provide it anymore."

They sat in the quietness of the living room. The children's voices from playing and laughter resonated outside the picture window.

"I love you, Emmy. I love you with all my heart. I know it has been unbearable at times these past five years, but honestly honey, aren't you just tired? Tired of fighting yourself?"

"Fighting myself?" she asked, confused.

"Emma Marie, it's our nature to love, to be loved. Why not, just this once, stop fighting and give love another chance."

She had composed herself, attentive to her mother's heartfelt words. She knew she was right and deep down agreed it was time to move forward. Even if Ken wasn't anything more than a friend, it'd still be nice to have someone to talk to and have dinner with from time to time. Was there a possibility for the relationship she had with Ken to grow beyond friendship? He'd already awakened feelings that hadn't been sparked for a long while. That spark was the foundation for her fears.

"By the way, just who are we talking about? Is he someone I know? Have I met him?"

Emmy smiled. "I know what you're telling me is right, but, Mom, I'm still frightened. It's not just about feeling guilty about Sean anymore. I have to think about Joy and what's best for her. What if he turns out to be all wrong? I don't know, maybe I'm simply afraid to love. I couldn't go through losing someone again, not ever."

"You have every reason to be scared my dear, but wouldn't life be just a bit dull if we weren't scared and unsure about some things from time to time? What would be the fun in a life full of certainties?" Her mother's arm reached over and brushed a piece of straggling hair away from her face.

"You make it all seem so easy." She grinned in spite of herself. It felt good to smile.

"Have faith my dear, the rest will follow. Now, getting back to my question that you conveniently didn't answer, do I know this gentleman?"

Her mother didn't beat around the bush and required an answer, reminding her of a five-year-old she knew and loved.

"No, not directly, but you have heard of him."

"You have my full attention."

Loud stomping of little footsteps entered the front screened-in porch. The fixed peering of round rosy cheeked smiling faces appeared through the closed French door windows separating the living room from the porch.

"Hi, Grandma Rothie! Hi, Mommy!" Joy's voice was loud and clear.

"Hi, Joy's Grandma Rosie! Hi, Mrs. Miller!" The neighborhood children echoed.

They waved as they smiled back at the beaming faces. She knew why the children were coming in, and only had seconds before they marched through the front door ready for their afternoon refreshments.

"I better go prepare to feed the troops. Thank you, Mom," she whispered. "I truly don't know what I'd do without you, I really don't. I just love you. Tight, tight hugs." She leaned over and embraced her mother.

"Tighter ones back," her mother replied. "And don't think I'm going to forget where our conversation left off."

Emmy set out freshly made chocolate chip cookies and mixed frozen lemonade with water. It slowly dissolved, along with her feeling of calm. Panic grew within. She stopped stirring. She glanced at the rooster-shaped clock hanging on the wall high above the kitchen sink. Her first date with Ken Kavanaugh was in a few short hours.

Whatever am I going to wear?

CHAPTER 10

Above all else, guard your heart,
for it is the wellspring of life. Proverbs 4:23

"Where we going, Mommy?"

While Emmy touched up her makeup, she turned to find Joy standing at the bedroom door. Sweet and angelic, she held her smiling red headed ragdoll drooped over one arm and her once-fluffy brown teddy now matted down from use in the other. She hadn't planned to tell her about the date yet. It was too soon. She didn't want her daughter to know about her relationship with anyone until she knew in her heart it was right.

"Come here you sweet little girl and give me a hug."

Joy ran over to her bed and carefully laid down her two prize possessions, double checking to be sure they weren't going to fall off the high double mattress. Then she scampered across the room into her mother's arms.

"Grandma Rothie ith fixing fried chicken tonight and it'th not even Thunday."

The gleam in her eyes and excitement in her voice made Emmy, for just a moment, wish she were staying home.

"Want to help me get ready?"

She still wasn't sure what her explanation for leaving that night would be. She wanted to spend as much time with Joy as she could before she left. The clock on her nightstand confirmed she had an hour before Ken's arrival.

"Where you going tonight, Mommy? Are you working at a party?"

Emmy loved working a party. During a catered event, she'd peek from behind closed kitchen doors where her desserts were prepared and soak in the glamorous details of the night, so she could share with Joy and her mother the next morning.

"No party tonight, honey. I'm seeing a friend for dinner. I shouldn't be too late." She finished her makeup, thankful for a simple explanation.

"Can you hand me the lipstick?"

"Here, Mommy. Can I put thome on when you're done?" Joy stood next to her and watched intently while she carefully added the final touches of painting on lipstick, stroking each cheek with blush, and adding eyeliner and mascara.

"Okay, honey, your turn."

Joy excitedly turned and stood with her lips puckered and eyes tightly shut. It was as though she waited for the doctor to give her a dreaded shot.

"Open your eyes, sweetie." Joy opened her eyes wide, and stood stiff as a board.

"Loosen up, honey." She couldn't help but chuckle. "Now relax your lips. Good. Ready, here comes the lipstick."

Her lips were so small the tube of lipstick was twice as big as their width. It only took seconds for the task to be completed.

"Now rub your lips together like something tastes really good, mmmmm, perfect. Now blot once like Mommy." She demonstrated by putting a tissue between her lips and blotting. "It's just like giving the tissue a kiss."

Joy took a tissue and mimicked her, amazed at the lip imprint left on the tissue. "My kith. Look Mommy, my own kith! Can I make another one?"

She was amazed how little it took to impress a five-and a-half year old.

"Can I keep your kith too?"

She handed Joy her blotted tissue, admiring her daughter's innocent youth and wonderful imagination.

Joy stood next to her, their faces reflected in the mirror. Joy smiled and leaned her head onto her soft shoulder.

"You're beautiful, honey, just like a princess."

"That's what Daddy uthe to call me, right? His princeth?"

"That's right, honey. You were his precious princess whom he loved very, very much."

Joy turned, wrapped her arms around her, and gave a loving hug. She prayed these precious moments would collectively sustain her as she continued to raise her child alone.

"Fe Fi Fo Fum," Grandma Rosie called from the bottom of the stairs. "I'm searching for a girl because dinner's done. Fe Fi Fo Fur, she better come quick or I might eat her."

Joy giggled in excitement as Grandma's voice got closer with each step.

"Where thould I hide, where thould I hide!" Joy searched the room frantically for a perfect spot. She took her arm and motioned for her to climb under the three-foot vanity. Joy quickly scooted underneath and slid back, shielding herself from view and giggling as Grandma Rosie entered the bedroom.

"You haven't seen a little girl come in here have you? She'd be about so high and is probably very hungry," Grandma Rosie said in a deep loud voice.

"Let me think. Yes, she was here, but if she was hungry maybe you should check back down in the kitchen," she replied, playing along with the game.

Joy giggled. Her patience with the game of hide and seek was always short lived.

"Here I am," Joy exclaimed when she climbed out from under the vanity. "Did you know that'th where I was hiding?"

"Well, you certainly are a little girl about so high, but I'm afraid I've never seen such a beauty as you before around here. What lovely lipstick you're wearing."

Joy laughed and excitedly handed over one of her tissue kisses. "Here Grandma Rothie, this kith is for you. It's mine, I made it."

"You made this kiss for me to keep?"

"To keep forever, Grandma, and it's not like the air kitheth, you know, the ones you blow and they dithappear. Thith one ith right there on the tiththue and you can keep it forever."

"I will, honey. I'll treasure it the rest of my days. Now come on beauty queen. Your chicken might fly away if we don't get back down there to eat it."

Grandma Rosie turned Joy towards the hallway staircase and sent her giggling on her way. Turning back, her mother asked, "You okay?"

She smiled and nodded yes.

"I'll keep Joy busy when he arrives and we'll keep out of your way. Just be yourself, relax and have a wonderful time. By the way, just so I say it enough, I love you."

"You can never say that enough. Love you too, Mom."

"If you have a good time tonight, I want a name in the morning, deal?" Grandma Rosie added as she turned to leave the bedroom.

"Deal," she nodded.

With those final words, her mother left the bedroom and headed downstairs to have dinner with her favorite princess.

She pulled a pair of brown penny loafers out of her closet and slipped them on. She was grateful for Ken's earlier call reconfirming their date and telling her to dress casual.

She sat in her room and practiced his arrival in her mind, envisioning his light blue and white DeSoto pulling up to the curb out front, watching him get out of his car and walk to her front porch.

She considered sitting on the porch when he arrived, but didn't want to come across as too anxious. Still, it would provide a perfect welcome without the possibility of introducing Joy to the situation.

She checked the appearance of her hair in the full length mirror that hung over the back of her walk-in closet door. She wished she hadn't gotten it cut so short at the end of the summer. It wasn't growing back as fast as she anticipated.

"It just looks so...bobbed," she fretted out loud.

She grabbed her rattail comb to heighten the top of her hair and made sure her bangs were even in front before she sprayed. One continuous push with her forefinger secured her strands in place while a fine mist encircled the air around her making it hard to breathe. Small pearl clip-on earrings her parents had given her when she graduated from culinary school accented each ear. She had decided to wear a beige pleated skirt with her light brown cashmere sweater decorated with pearl buttons down the front. A pair of opaque hose along with brown loafers completed her outfit.

"Brown. I'm too brown. Am I too brown? No, I'm neutral. That's good; I'm not making a statement."

One of Joy's big red bows sat on her dresser. She must have left it there earlier that morning when she fixed Joy's hair. She held it to the side of her head and examined herself again in the mirror. "Oh my, that would certainly get his attention."

She placed the bow on the dresser and again glanced at the time. Her heart began its familiar march. She checked in the mirror to assure its pounding couldn't be seen through her sweater.

"Oh, Emmy, you're hopeless," she blurted out as she examined herself one last time. "It's all going to be fine."

She quickly rehearsed her welcoming smile and practiced her greeting.

"Hi Ken, how nice to see you again. Oh hello, Ken. Ken? Is that you? Why Ken, you're so punctual. Good evening, Ken. Hey Ken, you look great, new belt buckle? Hi there Ken, love the boots. Kenneth, hello."

None of these seemed genuine. She had to be herself and have faith...the rest would follow.

With one last peek in the mirror, she glanced around the room. When she spotted the picture of Sean on her nightstand, she stopped. She needed an answer from him, a signal, some kind of positive acknowledgement what she was doing was okay. The only signal offered was the empty silence of their room. After a deep breath, she slowly walked to her bedroom doorway, glanced once more at his picture, and somberly turned out the light.

CHAPTER 11

With love, Heaven is there, also.

Emmy quietly tiptoed down the stairs, along the hallway, through the den to the living room and peeked between the closed curtains hanging along the French doors. She didn't know why she hadn't bought new curtains for the doors. Installed by the previous owners, they were old and wore the odor of musk. She must remind herself later to add washing the draperies to her spring-cleaning list. Ken's DeSoto was parked by the curb, but where was Ken? Searching up and down the marble stone path leading to the front door, she saw no sign of him.

Maybe he's still in his car. Possibly he's scared too? What if he changed his mind?

Then she saw him. He stood by the old oak and appeared to be studying the tree's branches, a lumberjack analyzing his next victim. She didn't know whether to wait for him to come to the door or go and join him. She dashed into the den, grabbed her jacket from the closet, placed it over one arm, and returned to open the front door.

"Here goeth nothin'," she quietly announced, mimicking Joy's words.

She guardedly strolled across the front porch and opened the screen door which squeaked loudly drawing his attention.

"Excuse me sir, do you happen to be lost?" She stood in the doorway. Their eyes locked.

The first sentence in a new relationship was always awkward. She was proud she got it out of the way fairly cleverly. She stepped off the porch, the door swung shut behind her.

"Not anymore."

His eyes glistened beneath the crisp fall leaves that shaded his face. His masculine features were even more striking outside amongst beams of sunlight.

"I'm sorry, I should've come right up to your door, but I got sidetracked by this gigantic oak. We have some big trees where I live, but I've never seen one this large."

He walked towards her, but stopped and waited by the tree while she made her way to him. The late afternoon sunlight created a sparkling pathway to follow in the front yard.

"How was your afternoon, Emmy?"

She grinned, surprised at his interest in nature and enchanted by his broad smile. If he only knew the uncertainty she experienced a few hours ago. Thank goodness for mothers.

"My afternoon was fine, Ken, thank you. Do you often get distracted by oak trees? It truly is a beauty, one of my favorites, too. Supposedly, it's one of the oldest in Cherry Grove."

"I wouldn't be surprised. The trunk is one of the thickest I've seen. I wouldn't be able to get my arms around it if I tried," Ken joked while he searched the oak's broad branches.

"Oh, but I'd love to see you try," she laughed, amused at the thought. "The oak actually fulfills many jobs for us around here and every season the jobs change. We couldn't be more impressed."

She drew closer to the tree—and Ken. She gazed up into the many welcoming, outstretched branches.

He reached up and gently grabbed one of the colorful copper leaves. "What career opportunities does this oak tree handle exactly?" he wittingly asked, carefully studying the leaf.

She smiled. Memories flooded back of the many times spent beneath the towering tree. She didn't want to start a deep conversation already, but since the oak had sparked his interest, she didn't think a little background would hurt.

"Many jobs actually, some of which I'm certain go unnoticed. As with all oaks, it provides shelter from the storms in the spring, shade from the sun in the summer, and as you've already noticed, provides vibrant beauty with its leaves in the fall. Look at all these magnificent colors."

Their heads were raised while they absorbed the reds, browns, oranges, and yellows silhouetted against the sky. A gentle breeze flowed through the branches and a crisp scent of fall filtered through the air.

Ken lowered his head and asked, "What about the winter?"

"So, you did notice I left that one out." She slowly moved around the large trunk and stood closer to Ken, drawn by his exquisite smile. She paused for a moment, carefully thinking of her response, and then said, "The winters are when we take care of him." She patiently waited for his inevitable question.

"And just how do you take care of an old oak in the winter may I ask?"

"You may ask, and one day," she paused to enjoy the moment, "I may just give you the answer."

She was surprised how comfortable she was around him already, like an old friend she hadn't spoken with in a while. His curiosity confirmed for her, that at least for now, she'd sparked his interest.

Ken drew one step closer. They looked intently into one another's eyes; renewed contentment made her assume for now he was intrigued with her answers.

"Are you hungry?" he inquired.

"Starved."

"Shall we go?"

Ken took her arm, sparking a warm and tingly sensation deep within and led her down the marble stone path. After assisting her into his car, he hurried around the front, noticing he stopped once to glance back towards the house. He grinned suddenly, as if he saw someone familiar. She quickly turned to see who it was, but no one was there.

She was anxious to know where they were going. In preparation for the evening and earlier anxiety, she'd totally forgotten to eat lunch. The sooner she could get wholesome food in her system the better.

"Where are we going for dinner?"

"We're eating at one of the county's finest restaurants."

"Finest? You did mention casual, right?" she quickly asked, worried she hadn't dressed appropriately.

"Casually the finest."

She silently sighed, feeling better about her choice of clothing even though self conscientiously she was as brown as Smokey the Bear. Glancing down at her lap, she inwardly groaned. Lying across her lap was her jacket—her light brown jacket.

"It's a little place about eight miles outside of town. I hope that's okay."

She needed to let go of her inner battle with color choices and concentrate on their conversation. She was touched by the politeness in his voice. She knew if she told him it wasn't convenient to drive outside of town, for whatever reason, he would've turned the car around and chosen a different restaurant closer to home.

"Yes, that's fine. The restaurant is eight miles out of town? Is it on Seawater Lake?"

"Yes, then you've heard of it?"

"It's had some wonderful reviews in the *Chronicle*. In fact, I've considered trying to contact the owner. There's supposedly a store connected with the restaurant. I'd like to see if they'd be interested in allowing me to sell on consignment."

She remembered reading the article about the restaurant's grand opening, publicized soon after Sean's accident. Although the event was highly talked about, it simply seemed insignificant at the time. She chose to stay at home even though her mother had suggested the venue as a nice place to go the evening following his visitation.

"Let's have our family and friends get together where there'll be no interruptions or further condolences for a while. You need to get away honey, if only for the evening," her mother insisted.

For a moment, her mind drifted to a time clouded with painful memories. An unexpected reunion with family and friends, some she hadn't seen since childhood. First cousins visited, second cousins reintroduced themselves while they offered deep sympathies. Close friends, fellow employees from the club, and community volunteers whom Sean worked with shared condolences.

Who are all these people? Why are they all here? Nothing made sense. Reality seemed elusive. She had wanted nothing more than to go home and hold her precious baby girl.

"Emmy, are you with me?"

She found it ironic her first date since Sean's death would be to the very restaurant she had avoided. It took a second to bring her thoughts back to reality.

"Emmy?"

"Yes, I'm sorry, what were you saying?"

"Have you been to the restaurant before?"

"No, but Chris, a good friend who manages the CGCC, has been there a few times. He and his wife, Mindy, always come back raving about the food, service, and especially the wine. He said they have a wonderful selection of vintage wines. I don't recall the name of the restaurant. How did you hear about it? Have you eaten there before?"

Ken braked suddenly. A thin, scraggly dog ventured directly into the car's path. "Poor little thing, he looks hungry. Get on across now. There you go, good luck to you little fella." The dog slowly moved across the road and trotted off in the opposite direction.

She stared at Ken with a warm approving gaze.

"What? So, I have a sensitive side," he grinned sheepishly.

"I can see that." She gave him a warm, favorable smile.

She was enjoying herself, and they'd barely gotten on the highway. Not every man around Cherry Grove would stop to let a stray dog pass, let alone talk to it, coaxing the poor animal across the street to safety. The barriers had started to fall.

"Ken, did you say you've been to this restaurant before?"

They were on the highway now with distant farmhouses on both sides. Some of the fields had already been plowed while others held their drying crop awaiting harvest. Colors of the trees shone vibrantly as the sun would soon begin to set in the west.

"I have. One of my favorite times is sitting out on the pavilion by the lake with a nice glass of burgundy and my own private viewing of the evening's sunset. It'll be perfect this time of year with the crisp, cool night air. That is, if that sounds good to you?" he asked.

"Yes, sounds perfect."

Again, she recognized his genuineness. She loved sincerity, especially coming from Ken Kavanaugh.

She was glad she'd brought her jacket, even if it was brown. She knew from experience growing up on the farm how cool the country night air could be. She suddenly wondered what he did for a living, but decided it'd make better conversation if she covered that question during dinner.

Instead, she kept it simple. They talked about the play and how well everyone had done. She appreciated Ken mentioning how cute Joy was as a sunflower, and how well she and Jesse played together after the play once they had cookies and punch.

"Jesse was exhausted from today. He was already asleep on the couch when I left tonight."

"I'm sure Joy was right behind him. It was a big day for both of them, for the whole class."

The car slowed down. Ken made a right turn.

"Hold on tight. They're going to have to do something about this road if they ever want to attract real city folk to eat here. Their fancy convertibles will be full of dust and dirt after driving a few seconds." He chuckled. "On second thought, maybe they should keep it just the way it is."

She laughed while they bounced down the road. Ken did his best to avoid the potholes, but even the deep ones, unfortunately, couldn't be avoided.

"I'm sorry about this, Emmy, but I promise the ambiance that lies ahead will be worth it."

"I believe you," she shouted above the noise of the tossed gravel.

The unpaved road lasted for about a mile. At the end Ken took another right onto a smooth two-lane street that wound its way along the east banks of Seawater Lake.

The water was calm and still as a sheet of ice. Several geese drifted atop its waters. Ducks quacked as they took off in flight, their calls echoing in the distance. They drove for a couple of blocks and rounded a final curve before reaching their destination.

The restaurant ahead was nestled between towering firs, large arborvitaes, and outstretched evergreens. It was as if heaven had opened its doors on the outskirts of a busy, impersonal, war-infested world and offered a private haven. It was the perfect escape from the real world, the ideal location for their first dinner together.

She gazed around the wooded area as Ken turned into the graveled parking lot. She immediately noticed the rustic sign perched above the large, wood-stained, double-door entrance.

Trusty's Restaurant & Ol' General Store

She wondered who Trusty was, hoping the story would be displayed on the back page of the menu once they sat down inside. The restaurant and store were connected by a long, narrow enclosed hallway. The north side of the restaurant revealed a wraparound porch.

The side facing the lake was furnished with colorful rocking chairs spaciously placed about, each one offering its own perfect view. *Trusty's* looked similar to a small cedar lodge one might find at a mountain ski resort.

"Ken, the restaurant looks magnificent. I can't believe I've never taken the time to come here before."

Ken opened her door.

"Very kind of you, thank you."

She inhaled, taking a deep breath of the fresh country air. The distinct aroma of fresh corn from the nearby harvested fields, evergreen from the assortment of pine trees, and wood burning from the neighboring fireplaces wafted past her. A line of smoke escaped from the chimney of the restaurant and another from the pavilion Ken spoke about earlier. The scents brought back memories of when she was twelve, standing over an open fire burning hickory nuts, pine, and cedar wood. She already felt at home and couldn't wait to bring Joy and her mother to visit someday soon, possibly on a late Sunday morning after church.

Her arm rested in his hand creating a warm chill within her body, a feeling that had lain dormant the past five years. She tried to suppress the sensation but it felt natural, welcoming, and for an instant she hoped he'd never let go. They walked toward the colossal front double cedar door. Ken pulled on the brass handle, holding the door open as they entered. It was as though they were entering a medieval fortress. The decor was as unique and stunning on the inside as the outside. Above were hanging chandeliers in the shape of wagon wheels. Accenting the spokes of each wheel were soft yellow lights that gave off a dim glow. The natural dark brown floorboards gave the appearance they'd been taken off an old barn wall.

Tables made of the same dark wood were topped with a shiny shellac finish providing protection from scuffmarks and scratches. The wood walls were a rustic, unfinished light brown and contained a variety of pictures. There were black and white pictures of avid fishermen, old men playing checkers on the porch, and women in ankle-length dresses playing croquet. Several frames showed veteran homecomings. Various photos of a white husky wearing a panting smile hung sporadically throughout the room and down a distant hallway. A faint romantic melody from the 1930's "Pennies from Heaven" played in the background.

Ken made his way ahead to the hostess stand as though to introduce himself and check on their reservation, but to her surprise there was no introduction. The hostess appeared to know him. He quickly turned, placed his hand on Emmy's back, which once again ignited warm tingling emotions, and steered her behind the hostess through the crowded main dining area to a table in an adjoining room off to the side.

A small table draped in a white linen tablecloth was elegantly set for two. The room had the same décor as the main dining area, with the addition of its own private fireplace that burned brightly near their table.

To the right was a large picture window presenting a view of Seawater Lake and a sunset-in-the-making filled with vibrant red, yellow, and orange. Two glasses of water and a bottle of Sterling Cabernet Sauvignon had been placed at the table. She was overcome with the natural beauty of the room and astounding view.

"Ken, I'm overwhelmed, this is stunning. The lake view is spectacular."

"Would you like a glass of wine on the patio so we don't miss the sun setting?"

Absorbed by the colossal colors of the sunset, enormous trees, and soaring wild life, she barely heard his question. Rarely did she have time to leave her busy life in Cherry Grove. She'd forgotten the serenity of country living, the simplicity it offered. Something deep within her awakened, and for a moment, she didn't want to be anywhere else. She closed her eyes to bottle the memory and then turned to face Ken who had an amusing grin. She wondered if he was bottling a memory himself.

"Did you mention a glass of wine on the patio? Oh Ken, would you mind taking the time? That'd be lovely."

Even though she had been ravenous on the drive over, food was suddenly the furthest thing from her mind. She strolled to the picture window while Ken nodded to the waiter to bring the wine out to the pavilion. He gently pushed open the sliding glass door. She followed him to the pavilion where they quietly sat and sipped their wine. The sunset disappeared, lowering its colors behind the horizon of the calmed water's edge.

The conversation was diverse ranging from religion to where she attended culinary school. She talked about her mother and the hardships she faced after her father died.

Ken spoke about his dad and untimely passing of his mother from cancer. Each subject was handled with care and respect. They learned more about each other's basic views, beliefs, hopes, and desires.

In the middle of the conversation, the evening patio air grew cooler, so they moved inside for dinner. She was so famished a shoestring would've tasted good. She inwardly reminded herself where she was and not to inhale her food.

And then he asked.

"What happened to your husband? Do you mind talking about it? If you do, I totally understand, I just didn't want not to ask," Ken questioned in the middle of dinner. He stopped eating and benevolently looked into her eyes.

For a moment, the ambience in the room made her feel she was the only person that ever mattered to Ken. Usually, she cautioned herself from answering questions regarding Sean. Every inquiry seemed too soon to discuss a subject so personal and painful. It was something she hadn't fully come to grips with even after five years. He waited for her reaction.

She put her fork down and wiped her hands on the napkin while she finished chewing a bite she'd taken before his question. It gave her time to contemplate her answer, if she even had one.

"I'll be honest, Ken. It isn't easy for me to talk about him even after five years. Unless you've experienced something similar, and I hope you haven't, it's hard for one to understand the feelings and emotions. I normally choose not to discuss Sean because...." she stopped, surprised at her truthful response.

She had said Sean's name to another man. A feeling deep within awakened as though the utterance of his name in some miraculous way brought him back to life, even for a second. Of this, she knew the impossibility. Taking a deep breath, she gazed at Ken and smiled. She wanted to be truthful; she simply wasn't ready to talk about Sean.

"Maybe if you began to open…," he started, but she motioned for him to let her finish.

"I'm sorry, Ken. Perhaps I can talk about it more another time. I can tell you one thing. He loved Joy very much and was a proud Daddy. He only had her for such a short time. When he died, it was as though a part of me died with him, and I've had a hard time getting that part of myself back. I'm not certain if it's even possible. Does that make sense?" She stared into his eyes, somehow already knowing he understood.

"It makes perfect sense. I could never imagine what you went through. You had to deal with your own personal loss while at the same time, learning to be both parents."

She started to pick up her fork but set it down again on her plate and leaned back in her chair. The hunger she felt before was replaced by a different kind of emptiness.

Let him know what you're feeling, Emmy. The words wouldn't come to share. Knowing she didn't have the inner strength to finish the conversation, she prayed Ken would change it to a simpler, lighter subject.

"I'm sure it has been a blessing having your mother around to help. I hope I can meet her one day. I've never been married. Spent too many earlier years learning how to climb into bunkers to keep quiet and watch. Like your husband, it's a subject I have a hard time talking about."

"You've been in the military?" She was relieved he had changed the subject. "Where?" She leaned forward and reached over and softly touched Ken's hand.

The waiter retrieved the empty plates. "May I present a dessert menu?"

Ken withdrew his hand and gazed across the table for her response.

"Thank you, but I couldn't eat another bite. It was all simply delicious."

"I was asked by the headwaiter to check with you, sir. When we're finished serving tonight, would you like one of us to lock up for you or will you be staying long enough to lock up yourself?" the waiter asked Ken.

Her curiosity awakened, she waited for Ken's reply and wondered if she'd heard the waiter correctly. If so, why would Ken be locking up *Trusty's Restaurant*? His facial expression switched from a concerned friend to a child who'd been caught with his hand in the cookie jar.

"You're new aren't you?" he grimaced as he asked.

The waiter, sensing Ken's irritation, cautiously nodded yes. He quickly gathered the rest of the empty dishes, put them on his tray and left.

It dawned on her after all they'd talked about during the evening, she'd forgotten to ask Ken what he did for a living.

"This is *your* restaurant?" she shockingly asked.

Ken grinned half a smile and uttered his awkward laugh. He'd caught her off guard by his hidden vocation and now she waited for an explanation.

"My restaurant, well yes. Surprised? It's true. Guilty as charged."

There was an awkward silence. She was surprised with herself. She wasn't upset by the fact he didn't tell her, but extremely curious as to why.

"Look, if I'd told you the restaurant was mine, you might have said that you loved everything, just to be nice. I was going to tell you right when we got here, but you were truly excited and sincere about how much you loved the place. I didn't want to break the magic.

"You see, I was thrilled with how pleased you were about the restaurant, lake, view, even the cabernet. I've enjoyed getting to know you. As the evening continued, on the pavilion and during dinner, I guess I simply—forgot." He paused to study her reaction. "I'm in trouble, right?"

She smirked and slowly shook her head. She understood his reason for not telling her and was relieved she truly loved the restaurant. How awkward would it have been if her feelings had been the opposite? His facial expression now resembled a whipped puppy, so she decided to let him off the hook.

"Well, Mr. Kavanaugh, I'm not sure I agree with your tactics, but I do understand. You realize I repeat myself when I say I absolutely love it here." She looked around the candlelit room, noticing a number of old photos framed in barn copse, and an antique wooden rake without a handle hung between the photos with a vintage bottle of wine settled on its toothed bar.

"You have something unique, endearing, and special. However did you find this place? Was it a restaurant before?"

"Thanks for understanding, Emmy. I should've told you straight out, but I wasn't sure how the night would...I guess I didn't want to give away too much of myself off the bat. Your honest opinion has truly meant something to me."

She wasn't certain where the night would lead either, but was pleased with his answer.

"Next time you want my innermost thoughts all you have to do is ask, but I'm warning you, my mother says I'm very outspoken when it comes to giving my opinion," she added. "Now Ken, tell me how you found this magnificent property."

"My parents started out with just the general store thirty years ago. You saw it when we pulled into the parking lot. It was built to serve the small community of folks that lived on and around Seawater Lake. The small general store, because of its wide expanding porch, became a gathering place to play games like chess and checkers, share fishing tales, and compare the size of the day's biggest catch. During hunting season, deer, duck, and pheasant stories took precedence. A few boaters and hunters from around the lake made it their routine to drop by and anchor their small boats at the wooden pier in front of the pavilion. After my mom passed away, my dad, Al, slowly built the restaurant addition himself. Kept him busy and his mind off things, ya know?"

She listened. Ken tightened his folded hands that rested on the table in front of her. Perhaps the memory of his mother's death captured his emotions as Sean's did hers.

"*Trusty's Restaurant & Ol' General Store* opened four years later and, well, here we are today."

Ken appeared uncertain as if he needed to explain further. Maybe he was discomfited or embarrassed by not sharing the truth about the restaurant from the beginning. She wasn't certain, but craved to know more about him and his history growing up in such an enchanting environment.

She leaned forward and gazed into his eyes, carefully sizing him up. "So, who is he?"

"Who?"

"Trusty."

"Ah, yes, Trusty. Trusty was the name of our old family dog. His full name was Trustopher, of course, and if he was really in trouble we would holler, Trustophiticus."

She laughed in amusement at the name.

"Trusty helped raise me. My mom used to tell me when I was little all she had to do was look for Trusty, and she wouldn't find me too far away. He kept an eye on me, followed me everywhere, protected me. Good dog, ya know.

"We were fortunate to have him the best of fifteen years. The night he died, that silly dog got up from his bed I kept in my room, and nudged my hand. It was hung over the side of my bunk. I was sound asleep; his cold nose woke me. I leaned over and petted his head and said 'good boy'. He lay back down on the floor next to me, closed his eyes, took one last breath and went to sleep. Kinda like he'd come over to say goodbye."

She hadn't blinked in minutes fearful she wouldn't be able to stop the tears that flooded her emotions. Thoughts of Fairway flashed through her mind. At the time of her greatest loss, she barely shed a tear for her fluffy white friend. He was a good little dog, a kind furry friend, Sean's constant companion.

He looked down and cleared his throat before he continued. "We built the restaurant over his grave. Kind of like a tribute to a job well done, ya know?"

No response was needed. Her silence said everything.

He brushed back his hair and swiped his nose with his napkin. Breaking the silence he added, "By the way, I own the restaurant, but my dad still owns the general store. He's getting on in years so he pretty much lets me manage them both since I've been back, well, at least for the past couple months. We both work with the staff and operation. I'll take you around and introduce you to everyone when we come back for lunch sometime. Deal? I'd like for you to see it during the day."

She realized this would make the second of two deals she'd made in the last six hours. She smiled. She wondered how her mother's patience was holding up back home, knowing she was dying to hear about her evening. He sparked many questions about his past, family, the restaurant and store. Had he been in the military?

She inwardly confirmed the questions could wait, answered when they returned the next time. Yes—the next time.

"I'd love to have lunch here. I'll take you up on that offer, Ken, and thank you for sharing your story about Trusty. I too know from experience, a dog is more than a pet as soon as you make it part of your family. That one awful day is worth all the unconditional love and wonderful days they give you."

It was late and the promise of a future visit made the departure more acceptable. They walked through the restaurant arm in arm, the old pictures on the wall now taking on new meaning.

As they neared the front door, Ken threw a set of keys across the room to the waiter who had served them. The waiter caught the keys in midair. "Lock up, kid," Ken announced.

"Thank you, Mr. Kavanaugh," he said excitedly, obviously relieved he still had a job. "Have a nice night, sir. You too, ma'am," the young waiter added.

They stopped for a moment.

"Talk to Cousin Joe if you have any questions. He's locked up many a night. He's pretending to work in the back room. Might need to wake him," Ken acknowledged since the waiter had a look of uncertainty in securely closing the restaurant for the first time.

The drive home went faster than she wanted, knowing the night would soon draw to an end. Ken helped her out of the car and walked her up the marble stone path to her house.

"We make certain it's not forgotten," she said as they approached the old oak.

She stood back and listened to the rustling of the leaves while the half moon, still bright, shone beyond the oak's branches. She sensed he didn't remember his question. The beginning of the evening seemed so long ago and they had shared so much. She focused her attention on the old oak and the memories it held of her past.

"In the frosty cold of winter after a fresh fallen snow, we used to make snowballs and pack smiling faces on the oak's aging trunk. Many faces smiled back when they drove by the frozen yards and frost touched houses in our neighborhood. Our family's Christmas pictures have always been taken right here. Even when the old oak had shed its leaves, it continued to provide shelter as we gathered in, watching us pose beneath its snow touched branches.

"Below, surrounding its wide trunk, nestled deep beneath the frozen ground waiting to emerge are roses of different colors. You see, my mother, Rosie, and I planted those roses the year Sean died. Our intent was for the roses to provide us, and the oak, strength to get through the winter, any kind of winter, with the warm simple promise of spring."

Ken leaned into her. She took his strong face in her hands and gently placed a kiss on his cheek. There was no need to rush. Their time still lay ahead. They embraced each other—it was nice—it was warm—it was good. Her hair brushed against his cheek. She stepped away leaving a faint scent of lilies amidst the air.

There was tenderness in his spirit, courage to give, and an instinctive quality she wasn't quite certain of yet. Above all, he projected a feeling of hope. She was at peace.

"Thank you, Ken. I've had a wonderful evening, more than you know."

"I have too, Emmy. Thank you for understanding, you know, about the restaurant. I'll call you?"

"Please."

They embraced once more, said goodnight, and walked in opposite directions.

She glanced back at the old oak, standing firm, witnessing their separation. Its silent stature and enduring strength of time held its own memories, hopes, and visions. Its roots were deep, long, durable, ready to welcome new birth. And now it held concealed knowledge—as if it already knew their future.

CHAPTER 12

...and roses will adorn her wedding gown.

"Ken Kavanaugh," Emmy announced loud and clear, as she stood in the doorway of her mother's bedroom. The sun was barely up and already the cozy room was brilliantly bright.

"Jesse's notorious uncle," Emmy added. She walked across the hallway and into the large galley-size kitchen.

Rosie lay in bed with her eyes open and whispered to herself, "So, that's his name."

She quickly sat up and crawled out of her warm bed, putting on wire-rim glasses, red-and-beige-plaid flannel housecoat, and fuzzy worn moccasins. She scurried into the kitchen to join her daughter.

The coffee percolated. She sat at the small wooden kitchen table nestled beneath the picture window overlooking the backyard. Emmy joined her.

"Ken was a perfect gentleman the entire evening, Mom. His family operates *Trusty's,* you know the restaurant on Seawater Lake?"

Nothing was more important to her right now than hearing about her daughter's first engagement with a man since that awful night five years past.

"Ken owns the restaurant and his dad owns the old general store which is attached to their restaurant. Ken manages both since he's been home the last few months. They have the most beautiful homegrown produce and it's full of foods and goods from local farmers.

"I can't wait for you to come with me to visit. I thought maybe on a Sunday after church. You'll enjoy all the knickknacks, and yes, they have fresh-baked items. I know how you love those. Maybe I can sell my own dessert creations there someday. I was going to mention the idea to Ken at the end of the night, but we found ourselves talking about the old oak out front."

Emmy's facial expressions came alive. There was an added sense of excitement in the way her daughter spoke each sentence. She found herself thinking more about what the future had in store for Emmy rather than what she actually said.

"I told him about the history of the oak. How we comment each season on its towering size, colorful leaves, warmth in the winter, and coolness in the summer. He was kind and even listened about the roses we planted. Most men would have darted by then." Emmy gave a heartfelt laugh.

"Oh, how you hesitated the year I made you help me plant those roses. Look what a focal point they became last night. Emmy, I'm happy for you, so very happy, Dearie." She sat silent for a moment, staring into her coffee, its steam twirled as it rose.

"Takes me back." The hot cup let warmth seep down into her aging fingers. She turned and twisted her gold wedding band snug on her left hand ring finger.

"You're thinking about Dad, aren't you?" Emmy asked.

She nodded. She gazed at her beautiful daughter and smiled. Emmy was not only her daughter, but her best friend. Being an only child, they always had a close relationship. The bond grew stronger after her husband's death.

Their past included many heartfelt discussions regarding giving up the family farm and land she so dearly loved. Even the thought presented an emotionally hard transition for her. She'd be forever grateful to Emmy and Sean. They did their best to make sure she was provided for, giving her a place to live, and financial freedom to travel and visit other family members who loved and cared about her. She realized how it had strengthened their bond as mother and daughter, a connection she knew would last throughout their lifetime.

"Tell me again how you and Dad met. I mean, I know you met by mistake or accidentally, right?"

"Emma Marie, how many times have I told you that story?"

"I know, but I love to hear it in your words. It had something to do with Aunt Lelia, right?" Emmy asked while she sipped her coffee.

The memory was as clear as the day it happened. She didn't stop herself this time from drifting back to an era long ago.

"It was a Thursday, May 13, 1930. Your dad was what we called a city boy which meant he lived in town. Oh, how I used to envy that crowd in school. Not that I wasn't appreciative for what we had growing up on the farm, but what we had was so little. Of course, as a child, I never knew it. Your grandparents never let on we were poor. There was always food on the table, a soft bed at night, and love and laughter to keep us warm.

"The Depression hit farmers hard, and we lost most of the money Mom and Dad saved for us kids. By the time I was in high school, there wasn't much left for anything extra."

"You mean you weren't able to go out to have fun with your friends? I can't imagine."

"Not at first, couldn't afford to. Lelia and I took odd jobs to help out. She helped Grandma sell and deliver honey to a number of stores. I cleaned and ironed for the Callaways, one of the more affluent families in town. You know, they lived in the house that's now Callaway Hospital.

"We also did quite a bit of babysitting and earned enough to help buy our clothes, school supplies, and of course hair bows. I loved picking out new hair accessories. I remember Mrs. Callaway sometimes gave me her extries, as she called them. She'd say, 'Rosie dear, here's a little extrie coffee, take it on home with you or take this extrie bag of sugar, I bought way too much.'

"I didn't want to sound ungrateful, so I'd graciously accept even though I knew she had bought extrie just so she could help us out. Why one day, I remember, she gave me one of her beautiful dresses. She said she didn't wear the dress anymore and I was to keep it for my very own."

"Oh, Mother, how dreadful, a hand-me-down dress? Did you actually wear it?"

"You bet I did and proudly too. It was the most beautiful dress I owned, pink with ruffles that gathered around the hemline of the skirt. I'll never forget her kindness. Her husband, Art, was the manager of the Cattle Bank downtown where Grandpa kept his money, what little he had. She told me she'd had the dress for years and was tired of wearing it but, between you and me, I'm certain it was because she'd stopped by the ice cream parlor one too many times."

126

They laughed in unison while sipping their coffee and nibbled on the warm cinnamon buns Emmy had just taken out of the hot oven.

"I'm telling you sweetie, times were hard, not like today."

"So, how did Dad come into the picture, being from town and all? It sounds like you came from two different worlds."

"Your dad had a friend, Chet, who knew Aunt Lelia. They played in the band at school. Chet wanted another couple to join him and his girlfriend at the spring dance that year. I happened to overhear Chet ask your dad if he could set him up with the Ross girl. I didn't know Chet, so I assumed he must be talking about Aunt Lelia. I heard Dad tell him he wasn't sure if he was going to be in town the weekend of the dance and he'd let him know later."

"Did Aunt Lelia know about the set up?"

"I'm getting to that part, just sit tight. So, the next day at school I was at my locker, coming down the hallway was your dad. Lelia didn't know anything about the setup yet and your dad, poor fellow, didn't know there were two sisters with the last name of Ross. I noticed he stopped half-way down the hall and spoke to someone who pointed in my direction. Dad caught me watching and awkwardly bent down to get a drink of water from the fountain."

"Oh—he asked you instead, thinking you were Lelia?"

She laughed, still tickled by the memory. "It just happened I didn't work that day after school, but poor Lelia did. So, I was the one conveniently standing in the hallway by my locker. I was innocently putting my books away when your dad walked up, nervously introduced himself, and asked if I'd like to join him at the dance. I was so shocked I said yes without even thinking. After I said yes, he asked if he could walk me home."

"Right then? He walked with you right then?"

"Aunt Lelia and I use to meet Grandpa downtown after school on the days we didn't work. He'd give us a ride home on the back of the truck if he wasn't carrying a load of lumber."

"Mom, this is so forward of you. I can't believe you said yes so quickly. You didn't even know him. Good for you," Emmy interrupted excitedly.

"Now listen, Dearie, don't think I didn't at least have an idea who your dad was at the time. His locker was down the hall from mine, which is how I happened to overhear their conversation the day before. He was also in one of my classes, though we never spoke. I agreed to let him walk with me but told him he wouldn't be walking me home but rather downtown where he'd most certainly meet my dad. Didn't seem to faze him a bit."

"It was fate—pure fate."

"I think you're right. We took our time that afternoon and talked about everything under the sun. I'd never really had a beau for long before, but this, even from the beginning, was different. It was like being with a close friend."

"And you never looked back, now that's a love story. Oh wait, what about Aunt Lelia? Did she ever find out? What about the other couple, didn't they tell her?"

"Just a second now, I'll get to that. Your dad and Grandpa hit it off right away. Why even that first day when they met downtown, Grandpa asked him what he planned to study in college. Back then, I was shocked to even know someone who was going to college. When your dad told him agriculture, well the next thing I knew he was riding up in the cab with Grandpa. I was by myself stuck in the back of the truck."

Laughter erupted in the kitchen, echoing off the walls and into the dining room. She put her finger to her lips indicating to keep it down for fear of waking Joy too early.

"The other couple? Oh yes, well, ironically they broke up before the date of the dance. As far as I know, Aunt Lelia never knew about the set up and for that matter, neither did your dad."

"You never told Dad? Why?"

"Quite honestly, it never came up. Everything happened so fast in the beginning. It didn't seem necessary. You see, the next day I was at home helping Mother with the baking. The doorbell rang which was always a treat since our doorbell never rang. No one ever made their way that far from town just to say hello."

"It was Dad."

"Now just a minute. The doorbell rang and we all ran to see who it was."

"Aunt Lelia too?"

"Yes, Dearie, Aunt Lelia too. In fact, she got to the door before Mother and I since we came from back in the kitchen. Standing in the doorway was a tall young man whom we didn't know. He asked if there was a Rosie Ross who resided here.

"I stepped forward and nervously told him I was Rosie Ross. I'll never forget the look on Lelia's face after he announced my name, oh goodness. He handed me a package with a note attached, then turned around and walked off the porch to a bike he'd propped against the railing, and rode away."

"What was in the package? Was it from Dad?"

"Yes, it was from your father."

She gently placed her rough hands on her daughter's and smiled. By Emmy's facial expressions, she could tell she was enthralled by their love story.

"Your father gave me my first pillow that day."

"Dad started your pillow collection? I never knew that, Mom. Which pillow? What did his note say?"

"The note was in his handwriting...." She closed her tired eyes and recited out loud as though engraved on the inside of her eyelids.

Dear Rosie:

This pillow made me think of you. Thanks for the walk, our talk and the ride home. Next time, can we sit together? Looking forward to the dance. See you at school. Charles

She opened her eyes and saw that Emmy's eyes had filled with tears.

"The pillow was small and white with a miniature single red rose hand stitched in the middle. It was the most beautiful gift I'd ever received, until we had you, of course."

"A red rose. Why, that's the pillow you always carry with you when you travel. Oh, Mom, a red rose for Rosie. What a wonderful romantic story.

"And even though his family had money, he still sought you out. He knew then you didn't need money to be happy. That's what Dad always used to tell me." Emmy sat close to the table with her elbows bent supporting her face in her hands.

She nodded in agreement. "I asked him once, a few months after we were first married, if taking over my family's farm would make us rich enough to live out his dreams. You know what he said to me?"

Emmy shook her head.

"He looked at me and said, 'Rosie, that all depends on how you define being rich.'

"I thought about it for a minute and decided I really didn't know how to define rich. I'd never been rich. Did I want a bigger house? Not really, the old farm house was plenty big.

"Did I want a shiny new car? Well, yes that would be nice, but we were getting by with the old truck just fine. Did I want more clothes? I never knew what it was like to have a closet full of clothes. I was fine without. I turned the question back around to your dad. I asked him how he defined being rich.

"He took my hands in his, gazed into my eyes, smiled, and said simply, 'To have enough.' I can honestly say to you today my dear, I've been rich my entire life."

Emmy stood up, leaned over and hugged her tightly, moisture dropped off her cheeks.

Later that afternoon, she ironed in her bedroom while Emmy finished the baking order for the YWCA Women's Group. Joy had been invited over to Debbie's house for an afternoon birthday party along with other children from their class. It was always too quiet around the house when Joy was away, but it did offer an opportunity to get chores accomplished without the help of a five-and-a-half year old.

A distant melody lofted tenderly from the transistor radio playing in the kitchen.

Emmy hollered out, "Mom, listen to this song. I think it could be about you and Dad."

The tune became louder and clearer as the words and music drifted into her room crystal clear.

The eve I met my lady,
my eyes I could not close,
Unless my dreams would take me,
to the gal I now call Rose.

She sang along with the familiar melody while she hung up newly ironed shirts and folded laundered aprons.

I saw her on the sidewalk,
walking into town,
She stopped to look into a store,
selling wedding gowns.

The doorbell rang. Emmy called, "I'll get it, Mom."

She knew each word in every verse. It was a song Charles sang to her whenever she needed her spirits lifted. She scuffled over to her dresser and turned on her own small black transistor as the melody began its second verse.

She turned and caught me staring,
Her smile soon appeared.

She strolled around her bed to her nightstand where his picture was displayed in an oak frame he'd made from wood off their old round barn. She picked up his picture and quietly sang the final line to him.

I parked the car and joined her
...we've been married now, fifty years.

"Mother look," Emmy exclaimed.

Startled, she turned. Emmy stood in her doorway with a smile so big it could've reached Alaska. Held out in front of her were a dozen gorgeous red roses. With her nose nestled in the blooms, she took a deep breath.

"They're from Ken. It's a sign, Mom. Red roses just like you and Dad. Aren't they just beautiful?"

"Yes honey, simply beautiful. Why don't you go put them in that glass vase with the dusted rose rim."

"You mean the one Sean gave me for our second anniversary?" she hesitantly asked.

"Yes, dearie. It will be perfect, don't you think?"

"I suppose it would be. Love you."

Grandma Rosie pulled the closet door open. She lifted up the lid to an old cedar chest that belonged to her grandparents before they traveled from Germany. It was worn and tattered from years of travel, now handled as though made of gold. She once contemplated refinishing but feared polishing the cedar would wipe away the history and stories. The ragged chest held her most cherished possessions. She took out the pillow wrapped in tissue paper and brought it to her bed. She slowly opened, just as she had when unveiling the package for the first time.

"All those years ago, Charles, and it's as if you gave it to me yesterday. You're always with me, honey," she said out loud, sitting on the edge of her bed.

She raised the faded old pillow to her dry lips, gave it a gentle kiss on the small embroidered red rose, and slowly placed it back within its wrappings.

She leaned over and turned up the volume on her transistor. Their song continued to play its familiar melody, as memories of yesterday recycled in her mind, like pages in an elegantly crafted family photo album.

CHAPTER 13

Simple things take up
the greater part of one's heart.

Colors of fall blanketed the ground as crisp cool air signaled the impending winter months soon to be arriving in Cherry Grove. The holidays were approaching, and although delighted with a number of new clients, Emmy was overwhelmed with the number of pastry, pie, and cupcake orders. Her mother helped as much as possible, but it became evident she needed to hire another set of hands if she was going to get the holiday orders completed in time for Thanksgiving.

She contacted a community college located near Cherry Grove. She was surprised when they referred her to the director of the Home Economics Department. Mrs. Forsten had attended a number of parties at the CGCC where Emmy often served her homemade pastries and was familiar and pleased with her unique creations. She agreed to meet to discuss her growing business and the possibility of sending a current student, enrolled in the Home Ec program, to assist her during the holidays.

"Yes, that sounds perfect, Mrs. Forsten. I'll see you tomorrow morning at nine. We can set up a schedule that will work for everyone. I thoroughly trust your judgment and anyone you might recommend. The sooner they can begin the better. Thank you, Mrs. Forsten. I look forward to meeting you."

She was beside herself with relief. If the student was a quick learner, she could assist with the baking or with deliveries which would be immensely helpful.

Later that same morning, she was in the kitchen sharing the exciting news with her mother. She knew she'd be pleased, as she'd recently suggested more help if she planned to expand the business to become more profitable. Her mother always made it a point to offer her opinion. Today was no different.

"Mom, don't you see? It's the perfect solution, a win, win situation. The students receive school credit by interning with us in our day-to-day catering operation and learn the business aspects, and we benefit with an extra pair of hands to help us out, maybe even four extra hands."

She strolled to the side porch door and peeked out the window. "No milk yet. Hmmm, I wonder what's taking Harry so long?"

She went back to the kitchen table and sat down to join her mother with a fresh cup of coffee before she picked up Joy from school.

"All I can tell you, Dearie, whoever they send to you needs to be a quick learner and able to follow directions for all the upcoming orders you've received. They need to be reliable, good natured, conscientious, trusting, honest...well, suffice it to say, you simply need another someone like me."

Laughing out loud, she almost spit out her coffee. She knew her mother was worried about her, concerned she wouldn't be able to handle the work volume and take of care of Joy by herself after she left in January for Arizona.

A loud knock sounded at the back screen door. She jumped up hoping it was finally the milkman. Harry was an older gentleman who refused to modernize his equipment for the daily milk delivery. Each morning he rode standing atop a red high- seated milk wagon slowly drawn through the streets of Cherry Grove by his white horse, Fred. Harry would climb off the wagon carrying eight glass bottles of milk in a hand-held wooden rack while he worked his way down the street on foot, delivering door-to-door. He always took time to talk and fill his customers in on any local news he'd heard along his route. During his deliveries, his faithful friend, Fred, would continue on his way and wait for Harry at the end of each block.

She was a regular customer on Harry's daily route. She loved to greet him and hear his story of the day which was always amusing. Her mother, on the other hand, found Harry to be crude, obnoxious, and avoided his visits as much as possible. Today was no different.

"Hi, Harry. How many bottles do you have for me today?"

She'd recently increased her milk order to three bottles, but Harry was getting on in years and forgot to adjust her order, bringing only two. She took it in stride, always amazed how he could forget a simple revised milk order, but tell you a story from thirty years ago as if it happened yesterday.

"I've got two down fer today, Emmy, but, well, if ya like one more, I've got one fer ya back in the wagon."

He was going on eighty—next birthday, or so he remembered. His years had been kind to him, but she noticed recently he was having trouble maneuvering his body in and out of the wagon. He was slower and less agile than she remembered when they first moved to the neighborhood. Knowing Harry, she knew he'd never give up his route easily even if it did require him to be a bit more fit and able. Despite his aches and pains, each morning he came with a smile; each morning he came with a story.

"Yer Mother here?"

Harry looked past her, probably in search of a familiar face that had already happily escaped into the basement to start the day's laundry.

"No, sorry, Harry, she's not available today." She wasn't good at lying. She felt the truth was written across her forehead in blinking neon lights.

"Good...crusty old woman. I do somethin' ta offend her ya think? Ah, you never mind. Got a story fer ya today, Emmy. Let me think here fer a minute. All right, yes, now I remember. By the way, did I tell ya I fell off a sixty-foot ladder jes last week?"

She immediately checked Harry over from top to bottom wondering how she'd missed seeing an arm, leg, foot or neck cast.

"Oh my word, Harry, what's broken? Were you alone and who took you to the hospital? Harry Adams, are you all right?"

Harry roared with laughter showing the absence of his two front teeth. She didn't quite understand his humor in all of this and waited, giving Harry a moment to pull himself together. He slowly bent down and placed two bottles of milk on the porch floor.

"I'm jes fine girl, jes fine. You jumped to conclusions there, Emmy. Ya didn't let me finish."

"You mean you didn't really fall?"

"Oh no, I fell all right, but cha' see I was only standin' on the first step."

His laughter was closer to a howling one might hear from a lonely pup lost in the middle of a darkened night. It was infectious, and she found herself giving in to his humor and joined him.

"Pertty good one there, eh, pertty good. Whew, that one done near tuckered me out," Harry exclaimed.

"Got a nother' joke fer ya sunshine. Let me think here, let me think, okay, here it tis. Fred's been helping me tell this one," he chuckled. "What do you get when ya cross a bull, a donkey, and a ram?" Harry raised his head and looked around making sure no one else could hear nearby.

Feeling she'd already been put through the ringer, she was somewhat hesitant to ask. She reluctantly repeated the question back to him. "What do you get when you cross a bull, a donkey, and a ram? That's a tough one, Harry."

His snickers were building; the gurgle came from inside his chest like lava stirring before an eruption.

"A nice big kick in the as...." Harry blurted out his answer.

"Harry!" She interrupted when she noticed Ken was making his way up the porch steps. His arrival was unexpected yet a pleasant surprise. From Ken's expression, she wasn't sure if he heard the end to Harry's unsuitable joke or not.

"Well, Harry Adams, hello! I thought that was Fred with the yellow straw hat parked by the curb. It's been forever since we've seen you at the lake," Ken said, extending his hand.

To her amazement, it turned out Harry was an old friend of Al, Ken's father. Al was an avid fisherman seen almost every weekend in an outboard motorboat on Seawater Lake. She stood back and listened as the two old friends became reacquainted.

"Well I'll be, little Kenny Kavanaugh. I haven't seen ya since ya got home from...."

"It's been too long," Ken interrupted. He gave Harry a brotherly hug and shook his hand.

"How about we make a Saturday of it sometime soon and catch up down at the lake. Dad would love it and so would I. You can even bring old Fred if you'd like. He can graze out in the back pasture while we have a couple of cold ones, maybe play some horseshoes," he added, patting him on the back.

"Oh, I like that ide'er, little Kenny. I like that very much."

She stood quietly on the porch, amused by their conversation, thinking to herself what a small world. Ken finally glanced over at her with a smile only he could give. She reciprocated.

She recalled their last embrace, the roses, and the movie they'd recently gone to downtown at the old Princess Theatre. Their time after the movie had been shortened. Joy was fighting the sniffles, and she wanted to be home in time to put her to bed. She wanted to be certain Joy didn't come down with something more serious.

Ken had spoken briefly about bringing Joy and her mother to the lake for lunch at *Trusty's* and although she wanted them to see the lake someday, she wasn't certain if it was simply too soon. For now, they were having fun and she wanted more time for them to get to know each other. As the two men continued in their conversation, she found herself selfishly wishing Harry would move on and continue his daily route.

"I was on my way over to the school to get Jesse and thought I'd check to see if you'd like me to pick up Joy too. I know how busy you've been. I could bring her here or, if you have time, we could grab a pizza for lunch and you could meet us over at Angelo's. What do you say?" Ken asked after breaking away from the conversation.

Normally, she would have thought going with Ken to Angelo's was a wonderful idea but, before answering, she glanced at Harry, the town crier. He stood between them soaking in every word uttered. He was now intently looking at her waiting for her reply. It would be all over town by morning.

As luck would have it, Ken turned his attention outside to the street.

"Harry, don't look now, but I think Fred might have pulled a walk-a-way." He let out his familiar laugh.

Harry stepped over to the porch and stuck his head out the screen door only to find Fred and the milk wagon gone.

"Dad-burn-it! Cane't take a dern second ta say hello ta enybody enymure. Dad-burn horse," Harry hollered.

"Come on old timer. I'll give you a ride back to the barn." Ken, still laughing, wrapped his arm around Harry as though to assure him everything would be all right.

Fred was impatient, plain and simple. He'd been with Harry for years and knew the many different routes throughout town. He'd wait for Harry in the sun, wind, rain, and if the roads were cleared, the snow.

Fred knew every turn, hill, stop sign, bus stop, and most likely where every customer lived. But he put his hoof down when Harry took too long telling stories, sharing a joke, or just plain talking too much. He'd take off walking back to the barn and wouldn't look back.

"Could ya, Kenny? That'd be real nice of ya."

When she bent down to pick up the two milk bottles, she noticed his wooden milk carrier and six bottles that still needed to be delivered.

"What about the rest of your deliveries, Harry? Can I help?"

Harry appeared frustrated, agitated, and confused. He took off his hat and scratched his head.

"Just tell me where to take these six bottles, and I'll deliver them for you. I bet some of them go to the McWard family down the street. Why they have six children last I counted, don't they Harry?" Emmy said.

She'd never spoken to the McWard family before, but knew Joy often played with a couple of their children when the neighborhood got together. She'd tried to meet them a few times, but always got the feeling they preferred keeping to themselves. She didn't want to pry.

"Why now, that'd be real nice of ya. Yes, here now let me think fer a minute. It's so much a routine ya know. Yes, four go to the McWards and the last two go to the two elderly gals across the road, you know, the sisters. One's real nice but that older one, Frances, well, she 'bout wants to knock my head off every time I try to say a dern thing. Trust me, her giddity-up, dawg gone it, got up and went. Derned old hag. The last two bottles go there, save yerself some ag-gre-vation, talk to the shorter one," Harry said. He winked and smiled.

They couldn't keep from chuckling at Harry. One thing consistent about him, you always knew where you stood, good or bad.

"I will, Harry. Now you two better get going if you're going to get to the barn in time to welcome old Fred."

Ken helped Harry out the screen door and down the side steps.

"I'll see you over at Angelo's, before you can say...Emmy Miller's Decadent Desserts," he announced with a smile.

She couldn't help but laugh, especially with the French accent Ken strongly placed on each of the four words.

"I'll call the school to let them know you're picking up Joy and to tell Mrs. Williams. Let Joy know I'll see her soon at Angelo's."

"Whoever came up with a name like that, dad-burn-it, what does it mean anyway? Did you say de-cen-dent? Hmphf, women," Harry bellowed to Ken.

She picked up the remaining six milk bottles to deliver promptly. She wanted to allow herself some time to freshen up before meeting them for pizza.

Her first stop was at the sister's home across the street. She didn't get a chance to meet the shorter one, as Harry called her. Frances was the only one home when she knocked at their door.

"Who are you, Missy?" Frances exclaimed in a gruff voice when she cracked open the door just wide enough for the door chain to pull tight. "If you're selling something, we don't want any."

The door shut, followed by the clicking of a lock being turned. She wasn't sure how she should reply, but was confident Frances would be thanking her in a few seconds.

"I...I have your milk. Harry, your milkman, had an emergency and I offered to deliver. I'm Emmy Miller from across the street. I have two bottles for you," she explained softly.

She patiently waited for the door to open, but it never did. Instead a note appeared underneath the door frame. She bent down and picked it up off the dirty porch floor.

The scraggly handwritten note read:

Leave the milk by the door. Tell scary Harry the next time he decides to play hooky, do it on someone else's route!

She left the milk by the door and guardedly walked down the steps to the sidewalk. She developed a new appreciation for Harry. She'd just met one of the reasons that had most likely added to his pungent personality throughout the years.

She walked back across the street to the McWard house carrying the final four bottles. She was glad she had the chance to finally introduce herself to the family.

The scuffle of many feet and the dog's low-pitched bark erupted as the doorbell sounded.

"Stay back, Greta. Sit. Josh, take Kenzie and go back and eat your lunch, Mommy has to answer the door. No, Greta, stay." A frantic woman's voice was heard as she managed the simple task of opening the door.

Standing before her was Mrs. McWard, holding a baby on one hip and using her left outstretched leg and foot to hold back the dog whose repetitive bark echoed louder.

"Hi, I'm Emmy Miller from down the street. My daughter, Joy, plays with a couple of your children." She yelled, hoping Mrs. McWard could hear her over the commotion.

Mrs. McWard remained silent as her oversized dark brown lab continued announcing her unexpected arrival.

"Harry, your milkman, had an emergency and I offered to deliver your milk."

Mrs. McWard leaned forward and took the milk bottles and crate. Two additional small children appeared from the side room. Each one took two bottles and disappeared down the dark front hallway. Mrs. McWard handed the crate back, thanked her and quickly closed the door.

She stood alone for a moment staring at the second door that had been shut in front of her face.

"Did that really just happen?" she said to herself.

She slowly turned to leave and walk back home. The barking continued until she was half-way down the street.

"Poor Harry, that man deserves a raise," she mumbled as she somberly meandered home.

~ ~ ~

"Can we come to Angelo's and have pizza every week, Uncle Ken?"

Jesse's hands were covered with pizza sauce. He ate his pizza by layers picking off the pepperoni first, cheese second, leaving the crust and sauce for last. He was currently in the middle of licking off the sauce from his last layer.

Joy was sure his mother would never let him eat this way, but Jesse had a unique manner of getting away with things whenever he hung out with his favorite, Uncle Ken.

"I'm not sure how well that would go over with your mom, Jesse," said Ken glancing across the booth at her mommy.

"Your handth are dithgusting! Uthe your napkin, Jethe." She, on the other hand, had no problem telling

Jesse what she thought about his manners, or lack thereof.

Ever since the incident in the classroom earlier in the year, they had found a happy medium with each other. Joy took a mothering role when it came to Jesse, making sure he stayed out of trouble, silencing him when his silly thoughts had found his mouth too easily. Although they would still argue from time to time, he was usually the one to back down first.

"Uncle Ken, I need another napkin."

Ken handed the red container of napkins to his nephew who proceeded to empty out half of its contents. He methodically wiped each hand in front of Joy, taunting her. Joy rolled her eyes, disgusted by his actions, and turned her attention to her mommy and her new friend, Ken.

She wondered why the four of them had gone for pizza in the first place. Jesse was just a classmate who she really didn't spend much time with. He was usually with the older boys he got to know from the previous year now in first grade when he hung around after school waiting for his mother to finish up. She knew Uncle Ken from the time he spent helping in the classroom, but couldn't figure out how her mommy knew him. It was time to investigate.

"Where do you work, Mr. Kavanaugh?"

Jesse proudly answered Joy's question. "He owns and manages the restaurant my grandpa built. Me, my mom, my grandpa, and Uncle Ken live on the other side of the lake from the restaurant and general store. My grandpa lets me have licorice whenever I want some...."

Uncle Ken cleared his throat and nudged Jesse with his right elbow. Jesse, growing an insincere smile yet clearly wanting to please his uncle, calmly added, "…and ask for it nicely, of course."

Jesse picked up another stack of napkins and continued wiping between each finger. She stared at Jesse for a moment while she thought over the information he so proudly proclaimed. He stacked his dirty wadded up napkins into the shape of a pyramid.

"You don't have a dad, Jethe?" she questioned.

"Yes, I have a dad. I have a dad, don't I Uncle Ken. Uncle Ken calls him Big Jack cause he's so tall. My dad is so tall he could probably touch the ceiling in here without even standing on a chair."

"Where ith your dad? Why haven't I ever seen him?" she cautiously asked. Something wasn't adding up regarding Jesse's father. She wanted to know more.

Jesse slowly hung his head down. She glanced at her mommy who gave a disapproving shake of her head, signaling her to stop with questions. Deciding to ignore her mommy for now, she glanced back over to Jesse who appeared to be conjuring up his reply.

"He's just not here right now, that's all. He's in, um, he's in Dang," he said despondently.

"Where'th Dang? Is it far away?" she asked, quickly looking to her mommy.

Everyone sat silent. She waited for an answer. Even Jesse stopped building his pyramid and pushed his uneaten pizza crust aside. The restaurant was filled with chatter, but all at once it seemed the world had stopped and everyone at the table, except her, seemed to know the reason why.

"Honey, Jesse's daddy is…," Emmy began to answer, but was stopped by Ken.

"Big Jack was here visiting just a few months ago, Joy. He flew all the way to Chicago and took a three-hour train home just to see Jesse and his mom. I wish you both could have met him. He wasn't able to stay home long, but we all had a wonderful time visiting during the two short weeks he was here.

"He's become quite the world traveler lately, but his favorite place to be is right here at home. You see, Joy, Big Jack is helping all of us for a while in a land and country far away from Cherry Grove. The place is actually called Da Nang. We just aren't sure right now when he'll be able to come home for good. In the meantime, I can guarantee you he thinks about Jesse and his mom every single day, right little J?" Ken explained.

"Those two daily thoughts are what keep Jesse's dad going and focused on the loved ones he's doing it for." He scuffed the top of his nephew's hair with his large hand making Jesse smile with admiration.

Ken paused for a moment. "He knows he'll see this guy again real soon." He looked down at Jesse and added quietly to himself, "I hope very soon."

She mulled over what was said for a minute. She didn't know different countries or the distance they were from Cherry Grove, but by the seriousness in Ken's voice and the look on his face, Da Nang must be very far from home.

"Ith your dad at the war? Is it the war that'th far away?" she asked.

Jesse slowly nodded his head yes. For a moment, there was silence.

"My dad's a pilot," Jesse proudly added. "When he gets home, I get to ride in a crop duster and fly high above the fields and spray stuff on the corn and beans. When he was home last summer, my dad said he might even let me help him land the plane. After that we're going hunting, fishing, maybe to a movie, wrestle together, play cards...."

She smiled at Jesse as he continued on the long list of activities he was going to do with his dad when he returned home. She didn't always like the way Jesse acted, nor did she agree with things he'd say that made her mad or got him in trouble, but she knew how hard it was not to have a dad. She wouldn't wish that on anyone.

Why wath there a war anyway? Why did people have to fight?

For now, as she looked across the booth and saw Jesse happily scoot closer to his uncle, she really didn't want to know.

CHAPTER 14

Leave nothing less.

Later the same evening, Emmy decided to turn in early. She looked forward to a good night's rest so she would be alert and ready when she met with Mrs. Forsten in the morning.

She quickly completed her bedtime routine of washing her face, combing her hair, brushing her teeth, and putting on face and body lotion. She climbed in between the cool sheets and soft quilt, one of the more extravagant purchases she'd allowed herself in the past few years.

She had first seen the brightly colored quilted bedspread draped over a lounge chair in the front window of Russell's Furniture Store located on Main Street downtown. She had enviously peered into the window several times while shopping with her mother knowing if she ever came close to touching the satin silky fibers of the fabric, she wouldn't be able to tell herself no. There hadn't been a single night she regretted her purchase.

She turned out the light and laid her head on her pillow, finally allowing herself to relax after her full day. As her body unwound in the warmth of her cocoon, her mind drifted to higher clouds where dreams were kept waiting.

"Mommy...Mommy." Suddenly, a faint distant cry came closer with each waking second.

By the time she opened her eyes and leaned over to turn on her antique floor lamp, Joy stood by her bed, breathless with tears running down her warm, pink cheeks.

She sat up on the side of her bed. Joy immediately climbed on her lap burying her head against her chest. She held her close as her small body shook deep within. She gently rocked her and whispered close to her ear, "It's all right sweetheart, you're all right, Mommy's here, Mommy's here, honey."

Grandma Rosie's concerned voice called from the bottom of the stairs, "Is everyone okay up there?"

"Yes, Mom, just a bad dream I think. She'll be fine."

"Love you both. Good night, sweeties," Grandma Rosie replied.

She checked Joy's forehead to make sure she wasn't running a fever and was relieved her head was cool.

"Did you have a bad dream, honey? Do you want to talk about it? Sometimes it helps to talk about it."

Joy shook her head no. She knew all Joy wanted was the love and security only she could give. They rocked while she thought of something to say to take her mind off her nightmare.

"Did I tell you Harry and Fred came by today?" She continued to hold Joy tight, selfishly wishing her child would always stay this small and loving.

"Let's see if I can remember the joke Harry told me. Oh yes, I remember now. He wanted me to tell you he recently fell off a sixty-foot ladder. Do you know how high sixty feet is, honey?"

Joy kept her head buried within her warm arms waiting for her answer. Joy loved Harry and Fred and missed seeing them since she started school. He told Joy he'd come by one afternoon after she lost one of her front teeth, so they could get their picture taken together. "Why, little sunshine, we'll be twins, we will," Harry told Joy.

"Not even a guess? A sixty-foot ladder would reach all the way up to the top of our house, isn't that high? But what Harry didn't tell me is he was only standing on the ladder's first step. He still fell off the ladder but not from sixty feet. Harry had a good one, didn't he?"

Joy remained motionless except for a tiny smile that emerged at both corners of her mouth.

"Wait a minute, what's this I see on your face? Is it a smile? You know I love to see your smiles."

Joy's smile quickly turned into a giggle. She sat on her lap pushing curls back away from her face.

"Can I sleep here tonight with you?" Joy quietly asked.

Her eyes glistened from crying and her nose badly needed blowing.

Emmy grabbed a tissue from the decorative box Joy had made for her in Sunday school, and handed it to her. Her daughter's small soft hands cradled her nose as she blew into the tissue and wiped before handing it back to her. She knew there wasn't a thought of throwing the tissue away herself. With any other child, she'd hesitate before reclaiming the used tissue, but in the past five-and-a-half years she quickly learned when they're your own, well, it might as well be your own.

"Climb in, sweetie."

Joy's smile stretched from one ear to the other as she climbed inside her bed and sank beneath its soft covers.

"Can we leave the light on tonight... in cathe Daddy comes back?" she sweetly asked.

Her heart sank when Joy questioned or spoke of her father. Oddly, Joy never mentioned him as if he had been here, as if he were still alive.

"What do you mean if he comes back, honey? Why are you asking about Daddy?"

Joy lay silent. Tears formed, dropping like raindrops down a windowpane. "I think you need to tell me about your dream. I know it's hard but sometimes, if you say it out loud, it helps you understand how the dream couldn't really happen and why you don't need to be afraid or upset." She handed her another tissue.

Joy wiped her eyes and stared up at the plain white bedroom ceiling.

"The dream was real, it did happen, Mommy. I was thwinging on a big tree thwing near a cathtle. The cathtle was white with big blue towerths and had a wooden bridge, the kind trolls hide under. While I was thwinging, if I pointed my toeth I could touch the sky, really Mommy I could. It made me giggle. I heard thomeone call my name. He was behind me. I thopped thwinging, turned around and there he stood. Daddy visited me."

She didn't move, enamored with her detailed description. She waited for her daughter to continue her enchanting story.

"He floated over the bridge to me thanding on a white puffy cloud. I couldn't reach him but I could thee him thtill. I'm certain he'd been in heaven, Mommy. He wore a pair of funny plaid pants made of all different colors, and a yellow thort thleeved thirt with a collar, the kind Chris wearths at the club. He didn't thay anything at first so I tharted talking.

"I talked and talked and he listened. I told him all about you and me and how much we mithed him. I talked about thchool and my friends, even about Jethee. I told him about Grandma Rothie being here with uth, and how your baking wath going to make uth rich. He smiled at me mostly but still never thaid anything. I thought maybe he had to wait until I athked him a quethtion, tho I did."

Joy turned her head towards her. She sat motionless listening to her daughter's beautiful and innocent description, unable to predict what her vivid imagination would say next.

"What did you ask Daddy, honey?"

"I athked him what it was like to be in heaven. I wanted to know if he thaw colorth, if he helped God paint the rainbows. I wanted to know if he could thee uth when he looked down. I told him I was still hith princeth and I liked it when he sang with me. I athked if he still loved and mithed uth. Thath when Daddy finally talked back."

"Sean, I mean your daddy spoke to you? Are you certain, honey? What did he say?"

She remained silent, hoping she'd remember every word, phrase, and detail of her dream. Her senses told her the dream couldn't be real but her heart hoped otherwise.

"Daddy told me, heaven is where your peace ith, Mommy. He thaid for you to find your peace and heaven would be there waiting. What did he mean?"

She used her own tissue this time to wipe away tears and blow her nose. She was taken aback by Joy's dream, and couldn't help but believe what she told her might actually be true. How could she have made it up at such a young age? No, it was just a dream. She cleared her throat unable to speak. She glanced at her daughter who innocently waited for her answer.

"I'm not sure what to tell you, honey." She thought the statement over for a moment. "Maybe he meant we need to find peace in our lives, peace in...."

Find peace in love, Emmy, and heaven will be there also.

She searched Joy's teary eyes wanting to hear more of her vision, needing to hear more, praying to hear more.

"Did he say anything else to you?"

Joy's soft locks of curly hair surrounded her head like a frame as she lay gently on what used to be her father's pillow.

"He said he'd alwayth love and mithed uth. Then a clock made a loud dong and he thaid the sound meant it was time for him to go. He slowly tharted to walk away on the cloud. I wanted him to thay with me, Mommy. I yelled, 'Daddy please don't leave, come back.' He stopped for a thecond, turned around and smiled. Oh Mommy, hith smile looked juth like hith smile in the picture by my bed. He turned back around and slowly walked farther away on the cloud."

Suddenly, Joy's expression changed as a sweet smile appeared and grew across her face.

"What is it, honey? What else are you remembering?"

"As he walked away, there was thith whithle. The kind Teresa's mother makes when she calls Tippy, her dog. I heard it again and again. Finally, I realized the whithle was coming from Daddy. Out of the cathle, a little white dog came running over to him. Daddy leaned over and petted him on hith head.

"The puppy was tho cute with curly white hair. It walked with Daddy and together they slowly dithappeared. That's when I started crying and ran in here to you. Why did he leave again? They went back to Heaven, right Mommy? But, I athked him to stay, why didn't Daddy want to stay?"

Joy's tears flowed. She held her close wanting to help her understand, even though she didn't understand herself.

"Daddy never wanted to leave you, honey, not even in your dreams. He never wanted to leave us. You have to remember it was a dream, it was just a dream."

She held her daughter tight within her soul, as she tried to throw some light on a dream full of questions.

She saw a little white dog? How could Joy know about Fair...no, it wasn't real, it was a vision, just a beautiful vision.

She tucked her daughter next to her within the warmth and security of her bed. She gently rubbed her forehead pushing soft curls aside and reminded Joy she'd be by her side the rest of the night. Within a few minutes, Joy was sound asleep.

She needed to get to sleep as well. When she reached to turn out her light, she noticed the light in Joy's bedroom shining into the hallway.

She quietly slipped out of bed and tiptoed down the hallway to her room. A small obstacle course lay in front of her as she entered Joy's bedroom. She stepped over the china dishes she played with earlier while sharing a cup of tea with Mr. Bear, picked up outfits and shoes scattered about, and gathered up slippers for her to wear in the morning.

Finally, she made her way to her nightstand where a beautiful pink and yellow lamp in the shape of a fairy shone brightly down highlighting the picture of Sean. She could almost feel the warmth of his presence. She reflected on Sean's beautiful smile that emanated from the picture, the same warm smile Joy spoke of in her dream.

Did you come to visit Joy tonight, Sean? I want to believe you did and yet, I know it's not possible. Is it?

The stillness of the room gave no answers. When she slowly reached down to pick up the frame, something had been inserted on both sides of Sean's photo. Holding the picture closer, she recognized what Joy had done.

Folded neatly within the frame were two tissues, one large, one small. Each held the imprint of a kiss.

CHAPTER 15

See how she sparkles and glows.

"When you're finished delivering the angel food strawberry cakes to the CGCC hurry on back, Ricky. I'll have the chocolate cherry rum cake ready to take over to the Women's Guild luncheon down at the lodge. It needs to be there by four."

Emmy Miller's Decadent Desserts was in full swing and Emmy enjoyed every minute. Her meeting with Mrs. Forsten at the community college paid off in high royalties when she sent over two top-notch students to help her during the holidays. Ricky, a freshman, had just turned eighteen. Sue was twenty and a sophomore. Both girls were enrolled in Home Economics. Together, they designed their schedules to accommodate her as much as possible. Ricky worked Monday and Wednesday afternoons and Sue worked Tuesday and Thursday afternoons. Both of the girls helped out on Friday mornings, but only if needed.

"Yes, Mrs. Miller. Chris is going to love these strawberry cakes. They're just what he ordered, light but with a strawberry flare. Do you care if Joy rides along?"

Both girls had taken a liking to Joy, which was another added bonus.

Thanksgiving was quickly approaching and although most orders would be completed in time for her to enjoy the holiday, she knew her endurance would be tested in the busy weeks that followed.

She decoratively placed fresh red cherries to complete the rum cake when the phone rang in the adjoining room.

"Hi beautiful, did I catch you at a good time?" Ken asked.

He always knew what to say to melt her heart. No matter how busy she was, time seemed endless as soon as she heard his voice.

"Hi, Ken, how did you know I needed a break? How are you? Has Jesse caught the prize turkey yet?"

Ken mentioned earlier in the week his dad was taking Jesse out to hunt for their Thanksgiving turkey. She didn't know when the big event was taking place, but she was certain she didn't want to be nearby when it happened. Hunting was never a pastime she enjoyed being a part of before, during, or after the innocent capture.

"No, Dad will most likely wait to take Jesse out the day before Thanksgiving. We love the bird fresh and soaked in brine before it's cooked. Makes the bird tender, don't you think?"

She used brine years ago when she used to pickle with her mother. Their cellar shelves were always full of relish, pickles, celery, and cauliflower. She was impressed Ken knew to use brine for cooking.

"Who gets the pleasure of skinning dear old Tom?" Plucking feathers from the warm body of an innocent bird was a sight she hoped to never see.

"Why, thought I'd invite you over to do the honors, Emmy. Good experience for you. The feathers come off along with the skin real easy, the bird hardly makes a sound."

She hesitated to respond. Ken's jubilant laughter echoed on the other end of the line.

"Very funny, you thought you had me, didn't you, Mr. Kavanaugh?" She waited for his joking confirmation, but his laughter stopped.

"Stop it Ken, I know you shoot it first." There was a prolonged silence at the other end of the line. "You do shoot it first, right?" She innocently fell into his trap without a second thought.

"Emmy, you really need to get back to the country more. Speaking of which, I think it's about time the three of you finally made a trip out here. What would you say if I invited you all out to our place the weekend after Thanksgiving? We have a guesthouse that provides plenty of your own space. I'd love for you to meet my dad, and I also want to meet your mom. We seem to keep missing each other. What do you say?"

Secretly relieved the plucked turkey conversation was over, her initial reluctance to respond was based solely on her busy work schedule. She quickly reminded herself Ricky and Sue would be home for Thanksgiving vacation, and she'd purposely left the weekend following Thanksgiving clear of any orders. Her mother had briefly mentioned a train trip to Chicago with her lunch bunch, a close group of friends she met every Friday, to begin her Christmas shopping. If it happened to be the same weekend, she and Joy could certainly use the break. A weekend at the lake would be a wonderful retreat before the holiday workload set in again.

"That sounds absolutely wonderful, Ken. Thank you for asking. Joy and I can definitely come. I just need to clear up a few things on my calendar. I'll check with Mom when she gets back later today and let you know if she's free to join us. You're sure we won't be intruding on family time? It is a holiday weekend."

She had fond memories of Thanksgiving being a special holiday weekend growing up on the farm. The entire family, grandparents, aunts, uncles, and cousins gathered for the fresh turkey feast. She loved having everyone together at home enjoying the simplicity of the farm. From the sounds of laughter of the women cooking in the kitchen, to the roars of the men playing horseshoes outside while enjoying a cold beer, all contributed to the celebration of their traditional holiday at home.

"You'll make my family time complete. I wouldn't want it any other way. I hope you can all make it work. Cathy said she's looking forward to having you come as well."

"I don't think I've seen Cathy since the play which seems so long ago now. I look forward to seeing her too and meeting your dad. I'll talk to Mom tonight and give you a call in the morning to let you know for sure."

"Talk to you in the morning, Emmy. Have a good night."

What an adventure Joy would have spending a weekend at the lake. She knew she needed to open up to her a bit more about Ken and the close friendship that had developed. She thought maybe tonight, after dinner, would be a good time to have their second family meeting.

Suddenly, she jumped up and ran back into the kitchen. Footsteps echoed off the side porch. It was almost four o'clock.

"My rum cake!"

~ ~ ~

"You mean Jesse's Uncle Ken ith more than an uncle to you, Mommy?"

Joy appeared confused when she tried to explain the newly developed friendship between herself and Ken.

"Joy, honey, Ken is Jesse's uncle and he's my friend, a good friend. It's not by accident that we all had pizza the other day. Ken invited us to join him and Jesse. We've been doing a few things like that together and I wanted you to know that I am enjoying his company."

Joy sat silent on the footstool in front of her chair and frowned. Her mind became puzzled trying to process what she'd been told.

"Mr. Kavanaugh, he'd like for you to call him Ken, has invited all of us to join his family at the lake where they live the weekend after Thanksgiving. Does that sound like fun?"

Joy crinkled her nose as if a scent protruding from a teaspoon of unflavored cough syrup wafted up her nose.

"Will Jesse be there?"

"Well, of course silly, Jesse will be there. He can't wait to show you around his yard. They have a big tire swing, a lake where you can both fish, and a beautiful restaurant with an old country store you can browse around like you love to do."

"How do you know all thith, Mommy? Have you been there before?"

This was no time to beat around the bush. It was time to give her daughter answers, and she was ready for her childlike inquisition.

"Yes, we had dinner at their restaurant one evening. It sits right by the lake where you can watch ducks and geese swim by and big blue herons. There are all kinds of wildlife that live there throughout the year. We'll have to remember to bring our binoculars."

She made it sound as inviting as she could, but she still wasn't sure it earned Joy's approval.

"Do they have french frieth?"

This was her toughest question yet.

"What? French fries, hmm, I'm not sure. But if they don't, I know Ken will make some special just for you."

"Mommy, does Mr. Kavanaugh, oops, I mean Ken remind you of Daddy?" Joy giggled and slowly climbed up and onto her lap. "It'th okay if he does, Mommy, I like him. I think he'th funny," Joy whispered.

She wrapped her arms around Joy and held her close as they rocked together in her chair. *Did Ken remind her of Sean?* It was too soon to consider such a question. *He does have his humor. He makes me laugh.* She smiled.

"I like him too, honey. Right now it's just different than it was with Daddy. We're still getting to know each other and important relationships always take time. The weekend will be good for both of us. We'll get to see how his family lives, and have the opportunity to do some things they enjoy and some we've never done before."

"Grandma Rothie tellth me when I try something different, I'm expanding my horizonth. Is Grandma Rothie coming too? Where ith she anyway?"

She could almost see her growing up before her eyes. *Expanding her horizonth?* Oh my, Mother, that's a big word to add to her vocabulary. She's only five.

"She's finishing up in the kitchen. We can ask her in a minute. In the meantime, you're happy with going to the lake? You'll be polite to Jesse?"

"I want to see the lake and feed the duckth. I can watch Jethee fith, but I don't think I want to touch one yet. He better not thart bothing me around, that'th all." Joy snuggled against her chest.

"I think you two will get along fine. We'll see how the weekend goes and if I find you have been on your best behavior, maybe I'll let you pick out something special from their store."

"The store his grandpa owns?" Joy excitedly sat up and winked, something she'd never seen Joy do before.

"Oh, I will be Mommy, just wait. I'll thow you, I promithe Jesse and I will have a great time. Do you think they thell jump ropeth at their store?"

Giggling, she hopped down from her lap and headed to the kitchen proclaiming, "Grandma Rothie gueth what? We're all going to the lake with Ken!"

CHAPTER 16

An injured deer, leaps high above all.

Emmy and Joy dropped off Grandma Rosie at the train station the morning after Thanksgiving. The rest of her lunch bunch had already arrived and greeted her as she slowly climbed out of the car.

Joy was as excited for Grandma Rosie's trip to Chicago as she was for her own. Joy jumped into the front seat and cranked the window down as quickly as she was able.

"Good-bye, Grandma Rothie. Don't buy tho much you can't carry it back home. I love you and mith you already."

Her mother and her five close friends stood smiling at Joy. Each one would have claimed her for their own.

"I love you too sweetheart. Be good for your mom and have a wonderful time. I hope there'll be another time soon when I'll be able to join you. Don't fall into the lake now, you hear me?"

"We won't. But I might catch a huge fith and bring it home to eat." Joy giggled.

"We'll both behave, Mom. You have a wonderful time. Find some good bargains and buy something for yourself for once."

Gertrude, one of her mother's oldest friends, bent over the car door window and gazed inside. She smiled and waved at Joy who had nestled herself back down in her seat.

"C'mown Gert. We've got us some shopping to do." Rosie took her softly by the arm and led her away from the car, turning back once to give a last wink good-bye as they walked toward the station.

"That's who taught me how to wink," Joy grinned.

"Thee you sssSunday," Joy proclaimed. She quickly rolled up her window and they drove away.

Joy chatted non-stop during the thirty-minute ride in excited anticipation of their weekend ahead at the lake. Joy tried to answer every question as best she could, but her attention was divided. She was challenged by Ken's directions, having only been there once.

"Is there a rope thwing? Will it be warm enough to swim? Can we go on a hayride? What about bugth and worms? Do you think there are sssnaketh? Will a bear come and eat all our food in the middle of the night?"

She wished Joy hadn't thought of the last question. She needed to calm her excitement down a notch before their arrival.

"We're just going to have to wait until we get there, honey. Ken or Jesse will be able to answer all your questions soon enough."

She followed Ken's directions perfectly. The scenery became more and more familiar. All of the fields had been harvested. Some of the surrounding acreage resembled a barren wasteland making one forget the fresh growth of crops they would surely bring forth again in the spring. She noticed the rustic sign along the highway stating *Seawater Lake, Next Right* and remembered the turbulent dirt road. She put on her turn signal. They were close. They bounced along the dirt road leaving a trail of dust from their wake.

"Joy, listen, don't be wandering off. Always be where an adult can hear you. Whatever they fix for meals, be polite and eat it, no questions asked.

Remember your manners. Use please and thank you and don't interrupt if an adult is speaking."

She had gone over the rules the night before. Joy appeared irritated she had to sit through orders once again. She was by far more interested in a large deer running sporadically through a recently gathered field, dodging itself between, over, and around broken corn stalks.

She returned her focus back to the road. A flock of geese took off a few feet in front of the car, flying over in perfect v-formation. Joy appeared spellbound. She quickly confirmed to herself her daughter hadn't heard a word.

"Joy, are you listening to me? I mean what I say."

Joy stared out the window as they made the final turn toward *Trusty's Restaurant & Ol' General Store* where they were meeting Ken and Jesse. The plan was to have lunch at the pavilion and then follow Ken to their house on the other side of the lake.

"Mommy, look how big the treeth grow. There's the lake, it'th so big," Joy squealed.

She smiled, remembering the first time she viewed the lake with Ken. Colors of the memorable sunset sent a warm and calming sensation through her soul, as if she were coming home after a long, unwanted journey. How wonderful it would be to live here, feel the serenity, and view the beauty every waking day.

"Trusty'th Rest...Resta, Mommy what's that word? Hey, there'th Jesse," Joy exclaimed.

She turned down the rock driveway and pulled up next to Ken's familiar blue and white car. She didn't think Jesse had noticed them yet. He was busy shooting a rock up into a tree with his homemade stick slingshot. She hoped they'd already devoured the fresh turkey that most likely met its fate earlier in the week.

"Now remember everything I told you and don't run off, we might be eating lunch soon," she reminded Joy once more.

Joy's face lit up. Her eyes followed something or someone behind her.

She quickly turned to find Ken standing at her car door. For a moment, nothing seemed important enough to matter anymore.

"Are you lost?" he asked through her window.

She smiled, imagining the warm embrace within his arms that surely awaited as soon as she got out. When Ken opened her car door, Jesse ran across the driveway to the passenger side.

"Joy, we're going for a boat ride. Come on, I'll show you my grandpa's boat. We rode over in it this morning."

Joy jumped out of the car in her new white tennis shoes, ankle socks, a pair of light pink pedal pushers, a t-shirt, and yellow sweatshirt. Her brown curly hair was in a ponytail, a white headband held back her remaining curls.

She quickly got out of the car and yelled for Joy to wait, but Ken sensed her approaching instructions.

"She'll be fine, Emmy. I told Jesse he could show her the boat, but he has strict orders to come right back. Cathy's down there anyway getting it gassed up. They'll be fine. Now, it's my turn. Look at me."

Her body relaxed when Ken took hold of both her hands and held her out from him at a distance. She'd taken extra time getting ready earlier that morning, wanting to look nice but not overdressed.

She chose dark blue pedal pushers with a white button down shirt, a soft orange sweater, and navy blue tennis shoes. Her hair was pulled back with a wide white cloth headband that allowed sprigs of hair to hang loosely in front of each ear.

"How are you? Did you have any problem finding us?"

Ken's blue eyes sparkled from the sunlight reflecting off the hood of his freshly polished car. Geese cackled on the lake. A fresh pine scent lofted from the nearby fireplace inside the restaurant.

Her bodily senses were overwhelmed, but none dominated more than the sight of Ken's welcoming smile. She sensed he was genuinely happy to see her. His welcoming expression showed deep affection, but she remained guarded, cautioning herself it was for her and not a preconceived conclusion of the time they would spend together this weekend.

"I'm so happy you were able to make this weekend work," Ken whispered as they embraced.

"I'm so happy you were able to make this weekend possible," she quietly responded. She was secure again. His arms fit snug around her small frame. He pulled her in closer, his bodily warmth wrapping her like a corset. She was safe and protected.

They held the embrace until the reverberation of someone's throat being cleared interrupted the moment.

"Are you two stuck like that or can I finally meet this gal I've heard so much about," a brusque, rambunctious voice uttered.

Al Kavanaugh stood a few feet away wearing a red Cardinals baseball hat, old worn jean overalls with one strap hanging loosely down, a pair of mud-stained beige boots, and a red plaid flannel shirt. He puffed on a Macanudo stogy.

Thin gray hair showed beneath the rim of his cap and the hairs on his unshaven face covered most of his thick leather-like skin. He leaned over and put out the stogy on the bottom of his boot and slowly made his way over to where they stood.

She turned and smiled immediately, noticing similarities between him and his son. Except for the years that separated their ages, Al Kavanaugh reminded her of Ken and his appearance on that first day of kindergarten.

"Sorry, Dad, I didn't hear you coming. Emmy, I'd like to introduce you to my dad, Al Kavanaugh. Dad, this is Emmy, Emmy Miller," Ken introduced, one arm around her shoulder.

She couldn't help but notice Ken's beaming smile during the introduction. He was ten years old all over again, showing his father his first-place prize in a 4-H competition.

She stepped towards Al to shake his hand, but he surprisingly didn't reciprocate. Instead he opened his arms and gave her a tight bear hug lifting her body up until both feet dangled above the ground. His masculine smell was a familiar one of tobacco and the fresh aroma you only get from working out of doors. Both sent her memory racing back to a simpler time when her mind was carefree. Al Kavanaugh smelled like her father.

Her dad had been a farmer. From early spring until late fall he worked outside in the fields, irrigating the terrain, plowing, keeping daily watch on the crops until their final harvest. He would eat breakfast before the sun rose and have dinner after it had set. There were days she never laid eyes on her dad but knew he had been in to say good morning by the scent that lingered behind. His masculine bouquet is what she held on to during those busy months until she could nestle herself once again upon her Daddy's lap.

"I hope that was okay with you darlin'. You're sure mighty small—we might need to fatten you up a bit this weekend."

She readjusted her sweater that had shifted during Al's strong embrace and quickly put aside emotions of her father's memory. She wondered if Al welcomed all of Ken's female friends to their home this way. He certainly was friendly, she thought, with a quiet giggle, maybe a bit overly friendly.

Al unexpectedly became quiet; perhaps he was gathering his thoughts, maybe sizing her up to see if she was going to measure up to his qualifications. She patiently waited, smiling, hoping to correctly answer his most penetrating question.

"Tell me now, do you like cooked squirrel?" he asked, plain and simple.

"Dad, I don't think she's probably ever had squirrel," Ken immediately answered.

"Oh yes," she quickly responded almost talking over Ken's protecting answer. "We often had squirrel growing up on my parents' farm. My dad loved to hunt and squirrel was an easy catch. Gnawing on the legs is the best, wouldn't you say Mr. Kavanaugh, much meatier?"

"You don't mind if I borrow her for a minute do you, Son? I knew I'd like this gal, I knew I'd like her all along. Now, how have you prepared the squirrel? I'm always looking for a new recipe." Al stepped in closer and put his arm around her.

She peeked over her shoulder. Ken was gawking at them. Although her overall focus remained on their weekend ahead, her immediate attention was clearly centered on educating his father on the most up-to-date varmint recipes.

"Oh, yes. I'll be happy to write some recipes down for you later. Of course, my mother is the true expert. She has a knack for knowing what spices to add simply by taking a quick sniff before putting it in the oven. By the way, she wished she could've been here this weekend and thanks to both of you for the invitation. In fact, now that I'm thinking of it, one of her favorite squirrel recipes has always been buttermilk squirrel pie, have you ever had any?"

"Why, no darlin', can't say that we have."

"Oh, Mr. Kavanaugh you're in for a treat."

"Call me Al now, you hear? I insist."

"Yes, Al. You're still in for a treat."

She turned and winked at Ken. The wink reminded her of Joy's earlier agreement to go to the lake, and she couldn't help but smile. Catching the scent of Al's cigar, she turned to join him. They walked off towards the restaurant and discussed grilled, slow-cooked, and stewed squirrel recipes until they were out of sight.

~ ~ ~

Ken stood alone quietly laughing to himself, joyous at the fact these two important people in his life had hit it off so well.

Did she say buttermilk squirrel pie? Just the name made his stomach queasy.

"That is not the way to a man's heart," he joked. His smile deepened, encouraged by what the immediate future might hold.

He believed in living forward, as he put the phrase. He never enjoyed reliving or worrying about events from his past. In fact, he didn't trust the past. Even in its certainty it held shadows that, if he let them, might affect his current happiness.

Yet, although he hated to admit it, he also knew, if he were to one day truly share his life with someone like Emmy, he'd need to unlock his past and share with her. He hoped she would do likewise. He wanted to know more about Sean, his interests, how he and Emmy met, the hopes and plans that filled his life—a life cut short too soon. He knew instinctively it was the memory of Sean that stopped her from truly opening herself up to another man.

He could hardly blame her—his own hurdle possibly too high and dark to share. He didn't want to burden her with his past, events that he still didn't understand. He wished they could remain buried forever. Or did he? Perhaps, if they gave themselves time, they would gradually grow to rely on and support each other. Together they could build a solid foundation of trust. Maybe then it would feel right to share their pasts, knowing whatever was said, the other would listen openly.

He knew deep down, they simply needed to love again.

He suddenly stood silent, almost frozen. A four-point deer stood in the middle of a harvested cornfield across the road. Its stance was firm, its shoulders broad, outspread, agilely awaiting its next surge. Both man and animal stood rooted as they scouted out the other's presence.

In his earlier youth Ken might have run to get his bow, but time caught both off guard while they stared intently at the other. The silence stretched between them, each daring the other to make the first move. The wind lay quiet, a cardinal's song was heard in the distance. Suddenly, without warning, a large flock of geese took flight from the adjoining field, their raucous calls startling the deer.

The panicked prince darted off, leaping higher with each gait, speeding across the barren field from left to right, disappearing into the distant horizon.

He turned and wandered back towards the restaurant to join the others. As he made his way, he silently remembered an adage his mother told him years ago. *Remember my boy; a wounded deer sometimes leaps the highest.*

"I wonder, I just wonder...." he quietly questioned.

CHAPTER 17

Close your eyes, open your heart.

The beautiful fall weather created the opportunity for one of the last rides of the year on Seawater Lake. Captain Al allowed Jesse and Joy to sit in the front of the ski boat as his first mates. Cathy insisted on joining them, one on each side of her. She knew her dad loved to drive fast.

As soon as Captain Al got to full speed, Joy and Jesse erupted into shouts of laughter as the wind and splashes of water hit their faces.

Emmy's worries about Al as a daredevil were confirmed when the boat hit every approaching wake head on, sending the boat into hydroplane mode for a few split seconds. She sat in the back of the boat with Ken, tightly holding his hand across the aisle.

Her face glistened from the warmth of the sun's rays reflecting off the water's crest. Her body nearly took flight as the boat bounced off wakes left by other boaters ahead of them maneuvering out of their path. Beyond the second crest she closed her eyes to feel the biting wind and occasional sprays of cool water land intermittently across her face.

"Emmy, open your eyes."

With Ken's soft shake of her hand, she drew her attention to the bow and couldn't help but laugh. Joy and Jesse had climbed on top of Cathy's lap fearing they'd be thrown from the boat. It was clear from Cathy's white-knuckled grip she was not about to let them go.

"Slow down, Dad," Cathy yelled.

Al was unresponsive to Cathy's cry. Sitting atop two life jackets allowed him to see over the front of the boat. Donned with a white sea captain's hat sitting jauntily on his head and an unlit stogy between his yellow aged teeth, Al appeared in his element.

"This boat is like a child to me, Emmy. Don't worry, I'd never put any of us in harm's way," Al bellowed confidently. "I have to warn you, after Cathy's cry to slow down, it only made me want to go faster," Al exploded with a boisterous laugh.

After seeing Emmy's pale face, Ken placed his hand on his father's shoulder and Al heeded Cathy's request.

"Sorry about that, Emmy, I got carried away. Everybody doin' all right?"

"Grandpa, that was better than the county fair roller coaster," Jesse announced as he released his grip from around his mother's neck. His flushed face told a different story. He sat next to his mother and took in slow deep breaths, carefully releasing them.

Joy giggled and bounced to the back of the boat plopping down next to Emmy. Her curls, loosened from her ponytail and headband, hung freely around her small, freckled face.

"That wath a wild ride, Mithter Kavanaugh. You thould drive a race car, I bet you'd win." Joy chuckled with excitement.

Al laughed. "Joy, would you like to come over and help steer the boat?"

"Can I Mommy?"

She gave an approving nod. Joy climbed onto Al's lap and took hold of the wheel. Al, keeping an eye on their path, took off his captain's hat and placed it on Joy's head. It dropped down below her eyes and

175

everyone laughed. Captain Al adjusted the hat to fit and announced there was a new captain today on Seawater Lake.

~ ~ ~

After the morning boat ride and tour of the lake, lunch was served in the pavilion. The unusually warm breeze blew through the screened-in walls and the delicious aroma of outdoor grilled barbecued chicken wings lingered in the air.

Joy was ready to nibble on a fresh ear of corn when, to her surprise, she spotted Harry, the milkman, slowly making his way down the steps of the porch from the restaurant.

"Harry. My Harry," she exclaimed, setting down her ear of corn. She ran towards her old friend.

"Well, I'll be. It's little Joy Who."

Harry bent low to the ground. She ran with open arms. Harry had been her confidant before she started school. She'd meet the milk wagon at the corner by her house and help Harry make deliveries up and down the block. She never noticed the way Harry talked different or the simple way he dressed. Harry told her once he loved her visits each day and what a sweet little girl she was, so different from the daughter he rarely saw or heard from anymore.

When she reached his outstretched arms, her excitement couldn't be contained any longer.

"Harry, I've missed you, I've mithed you tho much." She threw herself into Harry's arms and held him tightly as if never wanting to let go. His grip tightened around her. He sniffed back tears.

"What are you doing here, Harry? Ith Fred here too?"

Harry wiped his eyes with his white handkerchief and tucked it back into the hip pocket of his old worn blue jeans.

"Silly allergies...well I'll be, look how big you've grown, Joy Who. Why I betcha you're put ner almost as tall as Fred," he exclaimed holding Joy out at arm's length.

She stood back from her old friend and giggled in animation. Harry had always made her laugh, especially when he called her Joy Who. She was just three when her mommy started walking with her down to the corner of their street each day to meet him and Fred.

They enjoyed each other's company and having her join him on his route soon became part of their daily routine. The first time they met, Harry asked her name. When she finally gathered up enough courage to answer, instead of Joy Lou Miller, it came out, Joy Who Miwwer.

"I'm in thchool now, Harry. That's why I don't thee you anymore. I've really mithed you and Fred and your jokes. You been doing okay? Do you know Jethee and Ken?"

By now everyone inside the pavilion had noticed the special reunion taking place a few yards away.

"Well, I'll be—it's Harry. Joy, be careful and help Harry down to the pavilion," her mother called out.

"Now dad burn it, jest a minute dare folks, we'll be down when we're down. I haven't seen this youngin' in a coons age and we got some catchin' up ta do. Jest set tight fer a minute and gnaw on a bone."

She couldn't stop giggling and remembered why he held such a special place in her heart. She loved his kindness, his jagged walk as if one leg was shorter than the other, and his toothless smile.

"Harry, you lost another tooth. You were suppothe to wait for me. I have one tooth looth in front, wanna thee?"

She opened her small round mouth and wiggled her tiny baby tooth with her tongue.

"Well, I'll be yer right. Why I might be able ta snatch that out befer the weekend's over if you'll let me. It'll be gone fast as lightning, twon't hurt a bit."

She stood next to her aging friend and thought over his suggestion. It wasn't she didn't trust Harry. She didn't trust the inevitable pain she would feel when he pulled it out.

"Well, maybe Harry but Mommy thays we have quite a lot to do thith weekend. I'm expecting to be plenty busy. I'm not thure if there'll be time."

She decided to get his mind off the subject. Maybe he'd forget about her precious tooth, at least for the time being.

"I loved your joke about falling off that high ladder."

Harry seemed pleased when she took hold of his arm to help him. He slowly straightened his back and smiled.

"A high ladder did ya say there Joy Who? I don't think I've heard that one darlin'."

She took hold of Harry's rough and wrinkled hand. Heeding her mother's request, she headed down to the pavilion. She took baby steps, like the ones when playing red light green light with Bobby St. Cloud and the rest of her neighborhood friends. She didn't want to get ahead of Harry who seemed to have a difficult time walking.

"You remember, Harry, you've just forgotten, right?"

He slowly hobbled down the pathway to the pavilion, scratching his head as though trying to remember.

"Oh yes, siree, now I remember the joke, but why don't cha jest go ahead and tell me anyhows."

"You said you fell off a really high ladder, but you were only thanding on the first thep, remember Harry?" She excitedly reminded him of the answer.

Harry reacted as though hearing the joke for the first time. His jubilant laughter echoed across the pavilion, catching everyone's attention.

Al made his way up the stone path, greeting Harry with a firm handshake while patting him on the back. Even though Harry had a few years on Al, they'd been fishing buddies since they were teenagers. She thought it was probably good for Harry to see a friend his own age, someone stronger who could help him walk.

Harry waved a general greeting to everyone. Jesse ran up and gave him a hug. Harry turned to Jesse and her, both holding on to an arm. "Don't you two youngin's worry, I dropped Freddy boy off in the side pasture over by the house. You can both give him a juicy carrot later. How's that sit with ya?"

They smiled in anticipation.

After greeting Harry, Cathy instructed Jesse and Joy to take the dirty dishes from lunch up to Cousin Joe in the restaurant. They helped Joe prior to lunch shucking ears of corn and mixing ingredients used to make barbeque sauce for the grilled chicken wings.

"We'll see you tonight, all right Harry?" Jesse said while carrying a stack of dirty dishes.

"We're going to roatht marthmellowth around the fire pit, Harry," she added excitedly.

"Sounds like a grand time to me you two. Now get them dishes on up to Cousin Joe. Lickety split ya hear?" Harry laughed as he gave out his orders.

~ ~ ~

Al walked over, took Harry's arm, and whispered quietly in his ear. Without a word to anyone they nonchalantly strolled into the nearby tackle shed each whistling a private tune. Grabbing poles and a bucket of fresh minnows, they crept behind the shed to Al's johnboat and before anyone could question their whereabouts, took off.

Emmy and Ken began cleaning the pavilion. Cathy returned to take the remaining dirty dishes and silverware.

"You two need some time to yourselves. After I run these dishes to the kitchen, I'll take the kids to the general store and let them browse around for a bit. Afterwards, if you don't mind me taking your car, Emmy, I'll drive them over to the house," Cathy thoughtfully offered.

"I left the keys in the ignition, thank you," she replied.

"We have a big rope swing they can play on in the front yard. I know Jesse will want to let Joy see how high she can swing. Later I'll get them settled down for a quiet game of cards, or we can watch some old afternoon cartoons before tonight's big cookout. How does that sound?" Cathy continued.

"Perfect, Sis, gracias." Ken walked over and gave Cathy a tight hug around her neck, placing a loud kissing smack on her forehead. "Thinking of others first, as usual. You've always been the best at that." The brotherly affection was reciprocated with a squeeze around his trim waist.

"I'd like to show Emmy around this place a little more, let her get a feel for what our life is like out here, what we probably often take for granted," Ken continued. As they released their embrace, she caught the affectionate smile of hope and approving reassurance Cathy gave to her brother.

"Better yet maybe we'll take our time and walk over to the house. It's not that far, maybe a couple miles." He leaned close to Cathy's ear, looking off to the side at her. "Do you think she's up for it? Just look at her, like Dad said, so frail, so frail," Ken added in a loud whisper.

"Frail? After all I ate for lunch maybe we should run over to your house. Are you up for that, Mr. Kavanaugh?" she exclaimed as she walked over. She wondered how he'd respond to her challenge. She secretly hoped his original idea of walking to the house would suffice.

"Cathy, everything was simply delicious. You're quite the cook. Wish I could hire you."

"Believe me, Emmy, there are days I wish you could hire me, too. Ken, I'll leave Dad and Harry a note to drive your car home when they get back from catching dinner. Now listen, you two get going. The kids and I have all of the cleaning up around here under control. Go, enjoy—get."

Cathy took the hand towel, wound it up tight, and threw a big snap at Ken's leg. He jumped back and away from the towel, which barely missed him.

"Hey!"

Ken grabbed Cathy, pinning her arms and stifling her second towel-snap attempt. "All right, Sis! We're going already!"

She wondered what it would be like growing up with a brother or sister. Although she wouldn't trade anything about her childhood, their sibling affection was contagious. She watched, envious of their obvious deep bond.

In a few moments it was just the two of them, arms intertwined around each other, setting off towards the lake to walk the scenic two miles to the house along the water's edge.

CHAPTER 18

An unbounded memory.

Colorful fall trees were reflected in the quiet, still waters of Seawater Lake. The rustic beauty was breathtaking, unlike anything Emmy had seen before. For a moment she felt as though she'd been dropped into a different era only read about in books or magazines. An era where life moved at a slower pace and the rising and setting of the sun dictated the rhythm and activities of the day, not merely a morning signal to rise or evening's reminder to turn on the lights.

She felt relaxed. Her thoughts and emotions were freer than they'd been in a long time. She welcomed this time alone with Ken, and the opportunity it gave them to open up more. Maybe it was finally time to find the peace Sean spoke of in Joy's dream—time to start a new beginning.

Her expectations were high for the day and night that lay ahead. She was certain Joy was enjoying the weekend, and like her daughter, so was she. The early afternoon sun was warm on their faces, a soft breeze blew. Glad she had worn her wide white headband, it kept her ears warm and hair away from her face. She smiled for a moment recalling the earlier boat ride and wondered how unruly her hair was after Captain Al's wild jaunt around the lake.

After passing a few of the more prominent homes on the lake, Ken cleared his throat, breaking the silence. "I love this time of year on the lake, Emmy. It's so peaceful. It gets pretty hectic around here in the summertime. Many boaters are out and about, cruising by at full speed or drifting slowly close to shore viewing the residences. May sound surprising to you but, unlike my father, I personally enjoy the slower pace. In the summer I'll get up early, take the boat out by myself and meander down the various coves and byways, looking for a hidden lagoon or native wildlife.

"I remember one hot summer morning I came across a beaver lying on his back, sunning itself on a big flat rock down a narrow cove where I fished. Now when do you ever get to see something so unique if you don't get yourself out there to explore?"

For a moment, summer couldn't come soon enough, a time she wasn't exactly sure she'd even be a part of—yet. She tried to envision a much different scene on the lake and agreed with Ken, the slower pace was much more her style.

"Sounds relaxing, Ken. I love the freedom to explore and the lake definitely offers a number of ways to accomplish that. Like you said, the possibilities for adventure are endless. Do you enjoy one time of the year over another?"

They continued along the tranquil lake. Ken shuffled his feet along the bank kicking rocks that had made their way to shore.

"I love the crispness of the air this time of year. Normally, the cooler temperatures in November allow you to warm yourself by an open fire during the day and watch the flames flicker well into the night. Call me quirky, Emmy, but I love to stare into a fire, watching the orange and blue flames dance to their own music, a tune that seems to change by the minute." He closed his eyes and inhaled the clean air as if letting the freshness reach his inner soul before letting it go.

When he let his breath free, his eyes sparkled with a renewed spirit.

"You just can't bottle that smell, Emmy. If I could, I'd be richer than I already am, and I'm not talking about money." He took in another deep breath and released it. "It's simply enough, that's all you need you know…enough."

She remained quiet for a moment, remembering her parents and what they had talked about shortly after they were married. *To have enough.* A feeling of peace rose within her. *Was this a sign?*

"I can't believe how quiet it is around here since the boats have nested for the winter," Ken continued. "Guess the lake seems more serene. Winter solitude. It definitely allows a person to soak in their own private view and bless the coming winter days."

Ken glanced over at her as though to see if she was still listening.

"I got an 'A' in poetry, junior year English class, Mrs. Lane. I didn't want to scare you." He grinned at her.

"Poetry class, really? I thought you were a big jock in high school? You must've been bullied attending a class requiring such sensitivity and imagination. I must admit, your verse has certainly sounded spirited since we've been walking out here, Ken. Thought maybe it was because of me," she joked.

"Sorry, Emmy. Mrs. Lane had my heart for years. Her daily dose of rhymes always kindled my inner aspirations." Ken erupted with a heartfelt laugh.

She joined in. Although he joked about his poetic nature, she knew it was in keeping with a sensitive side she'd witnessed more than once. It was a side she was becoming deeply attracted to, a side that still frightened her.

A squadron of ducks paddled in a row around an old wooden dock puzzled by the scaffolding of supporting beams. One duck quickly followed the other as though tugged along by an imaginary band of elastic held by their mother swimming in front of the line. They scurried faster yet still in perfect form ignoring the human presence.

"They're looking for food and probably hoping we have some to throw out," Ken said. Ducks merrily swam across his casting shadow. "They usually hang around the lakeshore all winter and nest somewhere close. By spring they'll be ready to show off their babies. I must say they're pretty darn cute, as ducks go."

She noticed his soft blue eyes, how they twinkled when he'd caught her attention. He held a quality she always loved of Sean's; the natural ability to make her laugh.

"Sorry fellas, no food from either of us today, but you'll find a variety of bugs against the seawall at the old worn out dock on down the shore. Go on now, get'm while you can." Once again, she smiled as he gave formal instructions to his new group of friends.

It was his sensitive side that most intrigued her, however. The side that unknowingly showed itself, when he played with Jesse or stopped to let a stray dog pass, as if they'd been kindred spirits from long ago.

She yearned to know more about him and thought this might be a good time to bring up his childhood and past. After all, they'd agreed this would be a weekend to learn about each other and see what they were truly made of.

The mallards dove down under the water cleaning their flamboyant green, brown, blue, and orange colored feathers.

Her heart once again began its march. She conjured up enough nerve to ask her first question. "A mother is proud to show off her new babies, just like this mother duck, don't you think? My mom is a proud mother, I know I'm a proud mother." She paused knowing her next question would elicit a response full of beautiful memories or, her biggest fear, fall flat. She was ready to take the chance.

"I'm sure your mom was a proud mother too." She waited but he gave no reply. "Tell me about your mom, Ken. I know you mentioned she died from cancer. I'm sorry you lost her way too soon. What was she like growing up? What was her name?"

Ken remained silent. He picked up a flat white stone and threw it side arm across the surface of the water, skipping across low ripples. His stillness piqued her curiosity.

She guardedly continued. "Is it hard for you to talk about your mom, your childhood? I'd love to hear how you were raised, about your relationship with Cathy growing up and with your dad. You must be very close with all you've been through, what you've worked for, and accomplished with the restaurant and store."

His smile indicated she'd struck a favorable memory. A large rock lay before her. She welcomed the chance to rest while Ken found more flat pebbles to throw out toward the lake's horizon.

"I've lived on this lake most of my life, Emmy, except for the time I spent in the Army. I don't know anywhere else. Growing up as a kid was great out here. There was always a new place to find and explore, especially when you're little.

"Dad was always busy back then. He had to work more than a nine-to-five job just to make ends meet. He'd take me fishing when he could, showed me how to tie the right knots and put on the right lures. He was always mighty proud when I reeled in a big one."

He glanced across the lake. The cool breeze had quickened and she wished she'd thought to grab her jacket from the car. But she sensed he had more to say and secretly hoped they still had a mile or more to walk before reaching his house, allowing time for him to share more of his past.

"Dad was gone for a few years during World War II. My mom, her name was Annie, Anna Augusta Wood Kavanaugh, had to take over running the farm and store which was smaller back then, more of a hardware store. Dad's close friend, Harry, you know Harry, took over farming for us those few years he was gone."

"You mean our Harry, the milkman Harry? I had no idea his roots here went that far back." She smiled when she envisioned his toothless smile. "I love him even more."

Ken strolled over and leaned next to her against the rock. For a while, there was silence as the cool breeze blew against their faces. In spite of the chill, the sun continued to warm her on what was an unseasonably pleasant fall day.

"How did your mom hold up during that time? How did you and Cathy get along?" Emmy added.

"I won't say it wasn't hard. Those were tough times without my dad around to work the farm. But, my mom...." Ken paused.

She imagined his mother's memory captured a place in his heart meant only for her; the emotion in his eyes reached that special place.

"My mom was like this rock. Firm in her discipline, we didn't get away with much she didn't know or didn't eventually find out about, yet she'd melt like a marshmallow over an open fire whenever one of us thought to bring her a flower from the field, or left a picture we'd drawn—or simply told her we loved her." Ken chuckled at the thought.

"The refrigerator door was always full of drawings. I remember my mom telling me when I was small I never drew necks. I'd draw pictures of our family and none of us had a neck. After mom passed, Cathy found the drawings in a box under her bed. She'd saved every one of them. Guess those neckless pictures were some of her favorite memories. Crazy, huh?"

"I think your mother sounds beautiful. You have her sensitivity, I believe."

Ken despondently stood up from the rock as if he'd taken it one memory too far.

"Wind's kicking up, we should get going. I want you to have plenty of time to get settled at the house before dinner."

She slid down off the rock and stood up slowly, wanting to hear more. She wasn't ready to end the conversation. He was finally beginning to open up.

She followed behind him for a while enjoying the view and the different dock designs they passed. Some were painted in bright colors; others had upper decks built above the boat lift providing an exciting opportunity to jump off into the water.

Most boats had been taken in prior to the arrival of winter and the boats still on their lifts appeared old and uncared for. She caught up to Ken to continue their conversation. She imagined it had taken a while for his thoughts to reach back to his childhood. She wasn't ready to let him reel them in, just yet.

"Tell me, Ken, was I correct? You played sports in junior high or high school, after poetry class that is?"

She laughed, not certain Ken was listening. He'd stopped again, eyeing a couple of familiar fishermen who floated on the lake.

"I think it's Dad and Harry. Hope they're pulling in some big ones for tonight." He walked back to her and took her hand. His touch was soft, gentle, and caring and she felt it take hold of her soul. "Let's keep walking, it's not much further." She wanted to wrap her body in his warmth.

They strolled along the south end shore of the lake. She didn't think it could be much further.

"Okay silent Ken, I'll let you skip past high school for now, but I'm warning you. I have my ways of finding out about people. There are items called yearbooks that can tell an interesting story about a person, especially the personal messages written inside." One more question into his past couldn't hurt. She smirked as he mustered up an appropriate response.

"Two can play that game, Emmy. You hand over your yearbook, and I'll hand over mine, that is, if I can find it after all these years."

"When I see yours I'll hand you mine, not before. Deal?" She stopped in her tracks waiting for his reply.

"I can do that but on one condition. I insist we have dinner after we're done devouring each other's books, that is, if we can still stomach eating."

They had walked well over an hour but it seemed only to have taken minutes. They continued to share stories about their families. He chose a lighter topic and spoke endlessly about his close relationship with his sister, Cathy.

"I've admired Cathy since we were kids. As my older sister, she was always making sure my chores were done thoroughly and my dreaded homework was complete. After Mom passed she was forced to take on roles none of us anticipated. She did it without complaint all the way into adulthood.

"And now she's faced with another role none of us planned on. But she handles this one with that same optimism she had when we were growing up. She's determined to never allow her personal reality of raising Jesse on her own, while Jack is fighting in some far away country, to control her emotions. On the outside at least she seems confident and serene, certain Jack will one day be home. We all count on her being right. The alternative is unthinkable. I've always envied that confidence, her freedom from fear, her positive outlook on all things life has handed her."

"She certainly continues to amaze me even the little time I've known her. What a gift to have her in your life. What a gift for Jesse and Jack. I hope to meet him someday," she softly replied still uncertain of their future.

"I hope you will too," he answered. They stopped walking for a moment. He raised her hand and gently placed a kiss. She stepped closer and they embraced, their clasped hands snuggled tight between them. "You were an only child weren't you?"

"Yes," she said stepping back. "I know it sounds endlessly boring, but I never knew anything different. When I was little my dad and I were inseparable. He'd take me with him to check on the fields. We'd walk the

Cynthia K. Schilling

rows of beans together while he taught me songs and created stories that always featured one of our barn animals."

"You raised animals on your farm?" Ken asked.

"Oh yes, let's see there was Bessie the milk cow, Frankie the goat, and Dolly our horse. She even wore a straw hat with a long stemmed yellow flower. Really, she did. Dad used to tease he was going to pick me up in front of my high school one day riding her. I would've died of embarrassment." She chuckled at the memory.

"Sadly, he became sick soon after Sean and I were married. Mom tried to continue to work the farm. She loved it so. Her entire life history was in that house. She wanted to keep the farm operating, not for herself, but for the memory of Dad. He worked hard for many years trying to make enough money to save and retire early. Funny, isn't it, how life can take a tornadic turn in the opposite direction? Sean and I knew she couldn't run the farm on her own. Eventually, she knew it too."

"Life fortunately knew what you and Joy would need one day. All three of you are blessed," he said warmly wrapping his arm around her shoulders.

Their conversation continued easily, steady as the woodpecker's drill on a distant tree. They opened up to each other, finding themselves lost within the other's life.

"I entered culinary school right after high school. Is that when you were drafted into the army?" She slid the question in casually.

He'd stopped and looked out over the lake, possibly to clear his thoughts or ponder what to say next.

"You did say you were in the military for a while, didn't you?" She knew she was pushing but her curiosity got the better of her.

"I'm sorry, Emmy, yes I was in the Army. I was probably at boot camp around the same time you left for culinary school. It seems as though we were both trying to cook up something good for our future."

His laugh was forced, unlike the jovial chuckle she was used to hearing. She wished she could retract her question. She only knew a few people whose husbands or brothers had been called to serve. Of course, there were Gert's two sons, Hank and Henry. Gert was as patriotic as they came. Her younger son, Hank, was drafted and immediately afterward her oldest son, Henry, enlisted. She didn't remember where the boys were stationed or how much longer they had to serve, but while they were away she could always count on two American flags proudly flying from Gert's side porch.

Ken stopped to stare blankly out across the lake and the uneasy silence returned. She waited for him to explain his sudden quietude. A fisherman cruised by in an outboard boat and waved. They stood on the lake's shore, neither responded to his greeting.

She sensed a new unwanted distance between them. He had become guarded and she could feel an invisible wall spring up around him. She searched for something positive to say that would reignite the conversation, but too many questions took their place. She stepped back from him and surrendered to facts she couldn't control.

"Look, Ken, regarding the time you spent in the Army. You don't have to talk about it if it bothers you."

His continued silence made Emmy assume she was correct. "Maybe we should keep walking. It's getting late and Cathy may be wondering what's taken us so long. Ken? Shall we go?" she said, disquieted now.

Clearly in his mind he was no longer on the lake shore. Where was this place he traveled to, a place she couldn't reach? Gently, she put her arm through his and quietly led him in the direction they had been walking, hoping the distance wasn't much further.

Ken mechanically walked along side of her down the lakeshore until she thankfully heard familiar voices calling their names from a few houses away. Joy and Jesse ran towards them as fast as they could with Cathy quickly catching up from behind. She was relieved to see their approaching smiles bring an answering grin to his face. His sadness melted, as though a silent relief.

Unwittingly she had briefly touched on a part of his past he didn't want to reveal, a part that obviously needed mending. Whatever or whoever it was had certainly affected him deeply. She knew instinctively breaking through his reticence about his military background was going to be the key to understanding the real Ken Kavanaugh.

Her goal this weekend was to find out more.

CHAPTER 19

The Golden Hour
...and the day was no more and life soon was rested.

Upon arrival at the Kavanaugh home, Cathy showed Joy and her to the cottage where they'd be staying. They walked from the lake's shore up the grassy hill carpeted with red, yellow, and orange leaves swirling about the yard. Joy and Jesse ran from tree to tree trying to catch one as they fell.

She followed Cathy, noting although smaller, the burnt red cottage was an exact replica of the main house, complete with decorative flower boxes in each window. A large vegetable garden, dormant from the early frost and harvest, separated the cottage from the main house. A grey flagstone path wound its way down the middle of the yard allowing easy access to both residences.

"I hope you don't mind, but I took the liberty of bringing in your bags when I drove your car over. I left them inside the front door next to the spittoon," Cathy announced.

She was taken aback wondering why on earth someone this day and age would use such a receptacle.

"Don't worry, Emmy, the spittoon isn't in use anymore. Harry used it when he lived here years ago. Did Ken tell you? He used to help us farm when Dad was away during the war. I don't remember much from those days except for Harry's horsey rides," Cathy laughed. "He gave the wildest."

"Ken told me Harry spent some time here helping your family. He's a special breed, that Harry. Not surprising he gave great rides when one of his best buddies is a horse, Fred, the wild stallion. Joy, come inside and see the cottage where we'll be staying," she called across the yard. She walked through the front door and stopped with delight.

"Oh, Cathy, this is charming. I'm not sure what I was expecting, but after hearing Harry lived here, well I apologize, but I didn't expect much."

"I know what you mean. Dad and I redecorated about four years ago while Ken was away. *Trusty's* had been opened a full year and to be honest, Dad already needed something to keep him busy, keep his mind off things."

She was dying to ask Cathy about Ken's time in the military. Who would know best how to help him than his own sister. It must have been Ken's absence that worried Al at the time, wondering where he was and what he faced each day. He had to be fearful his son might not make it home alive.

Joy ran through the front door at full speed. Cathy immediately stopped her and asked her to go back outside and wipe off her shoes before coming inside. She quickly returned, shoes clean as a whistle.

"Thank you for all your help today, Joy. You'll have to tell your mom what we made, or better yet, let's surprise everyone later. Now, not a word you hear? Sshhhh." Cathy leaned over and gave Joy a hug. "You two take some time and get settled. I'll see you in a bit."

"Thank you, Cathy. I look forward to seeing the property and the main house. Let me know if you need help with anything." Joy walked over and stood by her. They waved goodbye.

"Bye Mrth. Hancock, thee you soon," Joy merrily added. They strolled back into the house. "Mommy, don't even try to get me to tell you what we made with Cousin Joe in the kitchen today, don't even try," Joy delightedly teased.

"I wouldn't dream of asking you honey. I love your surprises. Come on, let's check out the cottage and get settled." Joy appeared disappointed after hearing her reply.

The cottage was quaint with a small kitchen adjoining the even smaller living room which boasted a large picture window showing a spectacular view of the vast and awesome lake.

A short hallway led to two rooms, a small bedroom with twin beds on one side and a bathroom with a shower on the other. Standing in the hallway, she took the liberty to straighten an old photo hanging crooked on the wall. The photo was of Ken, who appeared to be in his teens, and his dad. Both wore an enormous smile, standing in a fishing boat, each with one arm around the other's shoulder, holding their fresh catch of the day.

Ken looked cheerful, carefree, oblivious to the difficult times that lay ahead. She wondered again if his military experiences caused him to be guarded and protective about that time in his life?

She continued down the short hallway and entered the bedroom only to find Joy bouncing from one twin bed to the other.

"We get to thleep in the same room, Mommy. You better not thnore."

"Now what makes you think I snore?" she quickly answered while she caught Joy in midair and fell with her on the bed laughing.

"Grandma Rothie thnores, I caught her. One early morning I was telling her that thory, you know about the porcupine that wanted to thnuggle and Grandma Rothie fell right athleep. I thought there wath a frog in the bed," Joy replied, giggling.

After helping to unpack their suitcases, Joy asked if she could go back out and play with Jesse, already at their screen door calling her name. She sent them on their way, scurried to the picture window and smiled watching them run down the hill. It was obvious their imaginations had taken over in play. Joy appeared to be having a wonderful time. She was relieved how well they were getting along.

When she turned her attention towards the main house, Ken was making his way down the path. She hoped he'd stop by the cottage, but he continued on the path without looking her way. She so wanted to resume their earlier conversation at some point, but resigned herself for now. Maybe it would be best to let things be. There'd be future moments, a quieter time.

~ ~ ~

A succulent dinner cooked over an open fire put the finishing touches on a near perfect day. Everyone enjoyed the fresh catfish Al and Harry had caught while they listened to two old friends bicker over who had the most difficult catch.

After dinner everyone enjoyed Joy's and Jesse's surprise pumpkin cupcakes, colorfully frosted with turkey designs. A crackling fire offered the opportunity for Al and Harry to reminisce about days gone by.

"Dad burn it, I was not sweet on Mary Beth O'Tool. If I had been we woulda courted I'm tellin' ya. Did she tell ya I was sweet on her?"

"Harry, you have too been sweet on Mary Beth ever since Dorothy passed on, God rest her soul. I can remember seeing you two out on your boat more than once, and I don't think you was just fishin'."

Al and Harry argued like brothers and did not appear to worry the disagreements would hurt their friendship. They'd been through both good times and bad. No battles, conflicts, simple disagreements, not even a woman could ever come between two men who'd been friends since what seemed like the beginning of time.

Joy and Jesse stayed busy placing marshmallows on freshly whittled roasting sticks, and delightedly watching them melt over the dancing flames. They'd raise their makeshift torch and blow out the flame, as if making a wish on a birthday candle. She smiled to herself. A sugar high would be affecting them soon, and they'd need a game or activity after their torch lighting ceremony was complete to run off their extra energy.

"Why, she still calls you her sugar. If that's not being sweet on someone, I don't know what is." Al and Harry continued their rant.

"Sugar, ha, she calls me that there when I sour up on her, probably wantin' somethin' as usual. Dad burn it, ya cane't jest go and sit with a gal enymore without evrerybody thinkin' you're wantin' somethin' permanent," Harry bellowed. "Is the sun over the dad burn yardarm, yet? This feller's thirsty!"

The fire began to die down, and Cathy announced she was going to search the yard for additional sticks and branches.

Her eyes followed Ken, who'd been noticeably quiet during dinner. He stood up and walked around the fire pit to where the other two men sat.

"Feel like a good old-fashioned game of flashlight tag, Harry? You know it was my favorite game back in the day. Remember showing me how to put the flashlight in my mouth and turn it on to scare Mom before I'd go to bed?" Ken took Harry's arm to help him stand. They laughed in unison at the special memory.

She loved Harry's toothless smile.

"Let's give it a try shall we Kenny? All rightie little J and Joy Who, not sure you two youngin's can keep up with me but I'd like to see ya both try. Where do ya keep the flashlights these days?" Harry questioned.

Together the four of them scampered away, Harry's arm in Ken's, Joy and Jesse jumping alongside in excitement. She hastily stood up to join Cathy in her hunt for sticks, but Al stopped her.

"So, let me get this straight, Emmy. You like to eat fresh meat and fresh fish, but you don't want to be the one to kill or catch it? Does that about sum it up?" Al asked as he stirred the fire trying to keep it going. He smiled, his sunburnt skin tightly fought against creases of his aging wrinkles.

"Just give me a piece of meat or fish to cook and I'll make sure it tastes good, but you got it right," she admitted, watching him across the open fire. "Don't ask me to watch it die, and then eat it." She had an idea where the conversation might be going and was ready to stand her ground. "You're actually in good company. It's a battle my dad never won with me either."

Al's smile showed the same glimmering twinkle that Ken's eyes had when he quietly acknowledged something she said amused him. They continued to watch the fire. Giggles and screams of laughter echoed off in the distant yard. Their conversation stalled, floating atop the fire as though waiting for the heat to spark and ignite questions that lay waiting to be asked.

"How many hunting stories has Ken shared with you recently? Did you know some of his best accomplishments happened before he turned sixteen?" Al asked.

She sensed Ken liked to hunt, yet he never spoke a word about it. Maybe it was because he knew she was sensitive to the sport or perhaps it simply never came up.

"Actually, Ken's never spoken to me about hunting, not that I wouldn't love to hear his stories. I suppose it's a subject for some reason he's chosen not to talk about," she replied as she looked over at Al.

She glanced back at the fire, uncomfortable under Al's piercing stare and what she suspected he wanted to ask, probably surprised Ken had never spoken to her about hunting and his passion for the sport. Maybe she didn't know Ken as well as she thought, but wasn't that what this weekend was for?

"Bet he's simply saving up his stories to tell me later," she suggested. "Was he a good hunter?"

Al's eyes were on her. She reluctantly met his silent stare. The sun stretched closer to the horizon and the reflections across the water cast flickering shadows upon his face. His thoughts seemed to lay deep within his soul, his mind, his heart struggling over whether they should be spoken. The evening's stillness enveloped them.

Al finally stood up, motioned to her and said, "Come up to the house with me for a minute, darlin'. I think it's time to show you something."

They carefully made their way up the flagstone pathway leading to the main house. As they passed the small, unlit cottage, she secretly wished she were already inside snuggled safely in bed with Joy sound asleep by her side.

Ken's uneasiness seemed to be growing and although she was certain she wasn't the cause, she did want to know why. Yet, at the same time, she didn't want to force the issue and chance ruining the weekend.

As they approached the house, they passed Cathy cautiously making her way back to the fire with arms full of tree branches.

"Keep the fire blazing, sugar, we'll be back in a few minutes," Al stated. He stepped onto the porch and pulled open the front door to the main house. The fresh scent of cedar wafted past her. They made their way through the large, oak framed door. Neither spoke.

The room was spacious, with walls and floors made of wood. A large, thick, rectangular rug carpeted the entrance to the main room. Dark brown worn leather furniture filled the living room, and was accessorized with deerskin lamps, a dark mahogany coffee table, matching end tables, a wet bar complete with a built-in sink, and a large stone fireplace that stretched across the far back wall. She followed him into the living room where he pointed above the fireplace to a mounted lifelike deer's head complete with antlers.

"Ken's first five point. He had just turned sixteen."

"Very impressive, it still looks alive."

She refrained from saying too much, knowing Al had his own reason for bringing her inside. He walked over to a long, reddish-brown built-in buffet on the left side of the room and slowly pulled open the top drawer as far as it would go.

The drawer was full of various colored ribbons, awards, and medals of different shapes and sizes. There had to be between twenty or thirty. She felt like an intruder. She leaned in for a closer look knowing Al was revealing a part of Ken she knew nothing about. She reached into the drawer and held a few of the medals in her hand, bringing them closer to read the small inscriptions.

1st Place Whitetail Deer/Still Hunting, 1954; 2nd Place Catfish Pull 1953; 1st Place Smallmouth Bass 1955.

"Do all of these medals and honors belong to Ken?"

"Just as I thought, he's never told you anything about his hunting awards or about winning any of these tournaments has he?" Al's facial expression showed his suspicions were confirmed.

She looked confusedly into Al's eyes and slowly shook her head no. The way he looked at her indicated there was something more he wanted to say. He slowly reached further to the back of the drawer behind the display of medals and brought out a silver key. Holding the key in front of him, he cautiously asked, "Has he ever spoken to you about...."

She waited for him to complete his question. Her heart rate unexpectedly increased. She sensed whatever Al was about to say was difficult as he searched to find the right words. Perhaps it had something to do with Ken's mother or his time spent in the military.

"I'm curious to know if Ken has ever talked to you about where he's been the past couple years?" he continued.

She stood motionless, speechless, wishing Ken would walk into the house to answer his father's question for himself. She said nothing and after a moment felt relieved to see Al's reassuring smile.

"Emmy, I'm not surprised he hasn't told you. He only talks about the past few years if we ask him and when he answers, it's brief. I think if I can at least clue you in, you'll have a better understanding of why he clams up or becomes distant and moody with you at times, like he has perhaps tonight?"

She wasn't certain she wanted to hear more. Whatever information he wanted to share, it should come from Ken, not from his father. He cautiously took the silver key and unlocked the second drawer of the buffet. She gently placed her hand over his to stop his progress.

Al turned and said, "You need to trust me on this, Emmy. It's something you need to know. Something Cathy and I both want you to know. Don't you see? Knowing will allow you to help Ken fight the demons he's unfortunately had to deal with these past few months."

She didn't understand what he was trying to tell her. What kind of demons could such a gentle man possess?

"Cathy knows about whatever this is, too? Al, he obviously doesn't want this brought to my attention and the last thing I want is to upset him."

Al probably sensed her frustration. He must miss his son, the son he nurtured, taught to fish and hunt—the son he once was close to.

"He doesn't want to deal with what happened, but he needs to and you might be his answer. We see how natural and content he is when he talks about you and when he's with you. You're the most positive thing that's happened to him in a long time. Please trust me on this Emmy, please."

She was touched by Al's words and the faith he offered to place in her. Still, she questioned why Ken had never shared incidents so strongly affecting his life, his happiness.

How would she be able to help him? What about her own demons? Her own scarred past and the inability to let go?

Al's eyes read a plea for help. Closing her eyes, she let go of his hand. Within seconds the key turned, the lock clicked, and the drawer opened. Slowly opening her eyes, she saw a drawer, again full of ribbons, medals, badges, and pins, but this time they weren't for fishing derbies or hunting achievements.

These medals were more sophisticated, authentic, and genuine. Her thoughts cautiously told her to stop—but her heart urged her to continue. As she studied the emblems closer, she immediately knew why Ken had traveled.

"He never said anything to me about…." She stopped. Her voice quivered. She took a deep breath. "Where exactly did he go? What happened?"

She picked up the largest medal and read the inscription, "For Valor." The ribbon was blue at the top and sides with red and white stripes across the middle. It held a bronze emblem of an eagle looking off to its side with its wide wings spread as if already in flight.

"That's Ken's highest award. It's called the Soldier's Medal. He earned it for putting himself in personal danger while voluntarily risking his life to save another's, a civilian."

Her mouth went dry. Her next question needed to be asked soon while her voice could still be heard. "What happened?" Her words came out in a whisper.

"Saved a little Vietnamese boy 'bout seven years old from his burning home. The boy's house was one of many huts on fire. The entire village was ablaze from the Vietcong who had gone through moments before Ken and his regiment arrived. The rest of his family was trapped inside the house. He heard the mother's shrilled screams and ran up a barren field to the house.

"Gunfire exploded around him. God only knows how he made it there and back alive. The mother quickly handed the boy to him through a window already ablaze and he ran back with him to his squadron. They held on to him, kept the boy safe. He started to run back to the house to help the others, but it was too late. The house exploded, stopped him in his tracks. Knocked him out cold.

"Both Ken and the boy suffered some pretty serious injuries. Ken's right leg was burned bad and, unfortunately, kept him from finishing his duty. They awarded him this Soldier's Medal and gave him an honorable discharge.

"He wasn't happy to go, a soldier like him never really is. They want to stay with their troop, their brothers. He felt he didn't deserve a medal for what he had done. Said the medal only represented the worst day of his life.

"Ken stayed with the boy in the Field Hospital while they both healed, even tried to bring him back to the states to raise him as his own, but too much red tape got in the way. Then one day the Red Cross found him, as the boy's uncle had been searching for the child.

"You can imagine how hard it was for him to leave the boy. They'd gotten pretty close during the few weeks they spent together even though neither spoke each other's language. The uncle, through an interpreter, thanked him for what he had done and tried to do. Confirmed to him the boy's name was An Toan, meaning safe and secure, ironic eh?

"When Ken was finally released from the hospital, he needed some time to clear his head, heal the wounds ya know. He traveled around Europe good part of a year. I think it kept his mind off what he'd been through, but even time couldn't clear away the memories. Since he's been home these past couple of months, I've often seen him up in the middle of the night with cold sweats. He tells me he's just hot and needs a fan, but I know what it's like to be hot. What I'm seein' is fear."

Al walked over by the large stone fireplace and brought down a large Winchester Ninety-four mounted on the wall above the wooden mantel. Slowly, he brushed the rifle with his hand as if clearing the cobwebs.

"He hasn't picked up his rifle or bow to hunt since he's been back. Says he's not interested anymore. You know I'm not so sure he could kill something again if he had to. He seems better the longer he's been home. We know you've had quite a bit to do with that, Emmy."

He winked and smiled, a finalizing gesture to his story. She took a deep breath to conjure up an appropriate response to the wealth of information she'd been handed.

"That explains it," she murmured quietly.

"Explains what, Emmy?"

"Why he wouldn't talk about his military career…I asked him it about today while we were walking. He fell into a deep, trancelike state. Tell me Al, did he enlist or was he drafted?"

"He enlisted as soon as he turned eighteen. Nothing could have stopped him. That boy chattered about serving his country almost since he could talk. Probably had something to do with hearing my war stories all his years growing up, probably made it seem more romantic than it actually was. His heart has always been soft, like his mom's. I worried about that when he left to go over, concerned he'd rather risk losing his own life than to take someone else's. Guess I was right."

She strolled to the front door which had a window with cross bars at the top. Peeking through the small pane, she spotted Joy and Jesse running circles around Harry and Ken, as if two helpless captured Indians. She followed Ken's movements and expressions.

She saw him in a clearer light and was drawn to him more than she ever had before. Al's detailed description of his son completed Ken's story, a story that helped connect the gap she felt in her heart, a gap she had been trying so hard to bridge. Now, she wanted to help Ken deal with the scars that had been left as much as she needed him to help her deal with her own.

"Love him, Emmy. I know you have your own issues to heal, but if you can both find a way to bandage them together I know you'll find…." Al stepped closer.

Startled by a commotion outside, she opened the heavy front door and quickly ran to see what had happened, Al just a few steps behind. Her first thoughts were of Joy. She was relieved to see her standing next to Cathy. Harry was already down the hill by the fire pit Cathy had obviously kept ablaze.

"What's going on? Where's Jesse and Ken?" Al asked.

They walked down the pathway closer to the others. It quickly became apparent no one was moving or speaking. They stood frozen, as if watching a dramatic scene in a suspense movie.

Al touched her arm signaling her to stop. He nodded in the direction the rest of the group stared. Ken and Jesse slowly moved towards a deer that was walking in circles near the bank of Seawater Lake.

"Does the deer not see them, why isn't it running?" she softly gasped as she turned to Al.

"Probably been shot or wounded. A deer will head to water hoping the water will soothe the pain. Unfortunately, Emmy, the water won't stop the inevitable from happening. The best thing Ken could do for the deer right now is put it down and end its misery. To be honest, I'm not so certain he's going to be the one to get the job done," Al quietly whispered.

Aware of Al's strong concerns regarding his son, she continued down the hill to join Joy and the others.

"Why don't I take Joy up to the house for a while until things have calmed down," Cathy whispered softly.

She acknowledged Cathy's good intentions to protect Joy from seeing what might happen. She leaned over and gave her a hug.

"Thank you, Cathy, you've been such a tremendous help to Joy and me today." She glanced in the direction of the deer. "What about Jesse, should he stay?"

"Jesse will be fine. He's been out hunting with my dad before and has a good understanding what probably needs to happen. Besides, Ken may need him to get through this. It's sad to see an exquisite animal on the outside knowing on the inside it must be in such pain."

Cathy paused for a moment to stare at the majestic deer, then turned to her and added, "You know, Ken may need you too."

"Come on honey," Cathy said to Joy. "I need your help to make this group some good old hot chocolate. Doesn't that sound warm and tasty?"

Without hesitation, Joy took Cathy's hand and headed with her towards the main house. They passed Al who was coming down the path with a rifle in one hand and a bow in the other. He stopped half way down the hill and waited until the proper signal was given to advance.

In the heat of silence, she grinned when she saw Harry, who had settled back down by the fire, softly singing to himself between hidden swigs of whiskey. Slowly, she made her way closer to Jesse who stood a few feet away from his uncle.

"Do you want your bow or rifle, Uncle Ken?" Jesse innocently coaxed.

Ken gave no response, but continued to stand motionless staring at the deer.

"It's been hurt bad, hasn't it? I can see it bleeding. Just tell me which one you want and I'll run and get it for you, okay?" Jesse whispered. His facial expressions showed desperation to help his uncle.

The sunset hovered above the horizon of the lake rendering a golden glow beyond the multi-colored leaves silhouetted against the sky. It dawned on her—

ironic a setting sun would parallel the solemn event that was about to take place. It was part of life's circle; she even understood why. What she had a hard time dealing with was the finality of the suffering target, and the fact it didn't know what was about to happen.

Jesse's patience wore thin. He walked up to his uncle's side and pulled down on his arm. "Uncle Ken, which one do you want?"

The deer struggled forward, making its way into the cool shallow water that covered the bleeding wound near its breast. She could almost sense the coolness of the water on her own body and imagined the soothing effect the deer must have felt.

The prince was out of its habitat in the water. She wished it was running free in an open field, leaping over high fences, or jumping across a flowing stream.

The deer stood chest deep in the chilly water and raised its head to stare into Ken's eyes. It made no attempt to flee, no venture to escape. It was as though the cool water that soothed its pain was worth more than freedom. The deer sensed they were watching by his twitching ears. She complacently concluded to herself, as tears swelled within her eyes, it also probably knew why.

The silence was suddenly broken. "No more killing, no more. Fire, I can't do it anymore; I can't see it, I just can't," Ken whispered to himself over and over. He buried his face in his large strong hands.

She moved closer to him, reacting to a natural impulse to help him in any way she could. His whisper for help spoke louder than a shout. She was overwhelmed with emotion, a wave of understanding for just how much she truly cared about this man. She stood silently, fighting the urge to wrap her arms around him.

"We have to Uncle Ken, don't you see it's hurt? It's hurt bad." Jesse instinctively walked closer to his saddened uncle. "We can do it, remember what you told me? Just like in my play, remember when you helped me, Uncle Ken? We do it. Remember? We can do it together." Jesse's echo of a similar conversation was both profound and moving.

Two souls looked intently at each other—one the older who loved and encouraged—one the younger, eager to learn from the best. Ken, although broken, tried his best to remain strong. He slowly walked over to his nephew, bent down, and hugged him with one arm, wiping his eyes with his other behind his small grasp.

She stood silent witnessing the scene. A vision of a screaming little boy being handed to Ken through a burning window rose before her. Certain of the child's fear, he carried the boy out of harm's way and handed the child to his troop for safety. Together they healed each other in the weeks that followed until they were strong enough to stand alone, protected, and secure. She recalled a less tragic but similar fear in his nephew when he stood alone, speechless on that school stage in a bunny costume. Unclear of his path, fearful he would fall. Once again, this man's quiet strength brought out the courage in a young boy, bringing him past fear and uncertainty.

"You're right, little J. You're absolutely right. We can do anything together can't we—anything." Although still visibly shaken, he smiled softly and scuffed Jesse's hair. A quiet hush fell. "I think it's 'bout time you run to the house and have Grandpa get my bow."

Jesse gave a quick hug to his uncle and an affirming nod and smile to his request. He pulled away from their embrace and ran as fast as he could back towards the house. Grandpa Al, who witnessed the heartfelt scene, stopped him in route to hand him the bow.

Ken's eyes found hers. They spoke in silence, words that only love could convey. She prayed he'd be able to finish the task set before him.

Jesse returned quickly, handed Ken the bow, and moved back to stand alongside his grandpa. No words were exchanged. No words were needed. They were replaced by a silent acknowledgement Jesse and his uncle were doing this together.

Everyone watched while the deer walked deeper into the lake until the water flowed up to its broad shoulders. The shot would need to be made soon before the water rose much higher. Ken slowly drew back the arrow and holding it in place—took aim.

In the blink of an eye, one heart ceased to beat. The evening light disappeared. The calm wind vanished. The once strong and mighty deer with its four point antlers slipped quietly beneath the water.

No one spoke a word. The silence signified its end. Ken slowly lowered his bow, and turned to find his father behind him.

"You all right, son?"

Ken closed his eyes and took in a deep breath. He exhaled. She could almost see the tension released.

"Yes, Dad, I'm good," he smiled. "I think I'm finally good."

Father and son connected with a long overdue embrace, neither wanting to let go. Jesse ran over to them and joined in the hug. Ken squatted down and met him at eye level.

"You did it, Uncle Ken, you did it," Jesse happily exclaimed.

"We did it, little J. Thank you, your help is exactly what I needed," Ken gratefully replied. He picked up his nephew and cuddled him close.

The once-mighty frame floated solemnly up to the still shore, its life now complete, its pain no more. Al left and returned with his truck, which he backed down the short slope of the hill to the lake. Together he, Ken, and Jesse reverently loaded the lifeless animal onto the bed of the truck. The silence wasn't broken until Harry, full of liquid spirits, unknowingly walked up to the group with staggering applause.

"Well, I'll be! That's quite a buck ya got there Kenny. Three point, eh or are there four or two? Ha, jes cane't quite tell in this here dark ya know. What time is it anyway? I didn't know you was huntin' again, good fer you. I knew huntin' would come back to ya, Kenny. As old Fred would say, it's jes like ridin' a horse."

All broke into a much needed round of laughter relieved the somber tone of the evening was broken. Jesse hopped into the back seat of the truck to help his grandpa take the deer down the road to Jake, a hunting friend who specialized in the cleaning and gutting process.

"You headin' on over to Jake's place, Al? Oh, he does a fine job, fine job. Where exactly did Kenny catch it? Why the poor thing's soaked, did it rain?" Harry hiccupped in between sentences as Al rushed over to stop him from losing his balance.

"I'll tell you all about it on the way over, Harry." Al smiled as he helped him into the truck. "Just put your head back and relax for a spell."

"You two go on back up to the house, get a nice bottle of that Cabernet I'm always bragging about and enjoy the rest of the evening. We'll be back in an hour or whenever we can wake Jake up enough to take care of this buck," Al instructed Ken and Emmy, who were standing close together now.

He turned his attention to his son and sincerely added, "I'm proud of you son, welcome home."

She wondered if Ken's actions had finally brought back a part of his soul, a part he'd left in front of that horrific burning home. She hoped what just happened proved to him it was time to let the past go and move on with his life. She was happy for Al. He'd finally found a small part of his son he feared he'd lost forever.

Together they watched the truck head down the road. She cautiously turned towards Ken, wondering whether to speak or let the comfortable silence continue.

He seemed to welcome the quiet. He took her hand and headed up the path to the main house. She felt safe with their hands entwined; his strength and warmth was what she needed right now. Hopefully, the tenderness from her hand sent back the same signal to Ken. The night air had cooled, sending a slight chill to her bones. It felt good to go inside.

She wondered if Cathy and Joy would be waiting with the hot chocolate as they entered the house. Her attention took a sudden turn when Ken released her hand and walked over to the unlocked buffet drawers. She stood motionless, cautiously anticipating his reaction.

He slowly turned and faced her. "You know…?"

He didn't appear upset. There was almost a sense of relief in his voice. He looked tired and drawn as if all his energy had been drained from the dramatic episode outside. Maybe he would look to her for reassurance— not an explanation.

"Yes, I know. Your dad told me earlier tonight. At first, I didn't understand why you hadn't told me, why you never shared such a significant part of your life. I can't imagine what you experienced, how you felt, the emotional questions that crossed your mind. Ken, I'm so incredibly proud of you. I pray one day you'll find peace with what happened."

"You realize I could say the same thing about you," he said. He slowly walked towards her. She smiled, grateful for his deep insight, agreeing with their similarities.

"If we could only continue to help each other reach beyond our shadows, our past, like you have tonight," she said. "I've always looked for signs to lead me, to tell me life is where it should be. When your dad told me about little An Toan, when he showed me your...."

Her voice cut off when he took her hands and brought her to him. His strong embrace made her feel safe and protected. She never wanted to let go. His hands explored her body when they traveled up her arms, across her shoulders, slowly reaching her face and hair, scouting every detail along the way. He traced each delicate feature as if creating a memory he never wanted to release.

"I'm sorry, Emmy. I should've told you earlier, but there was such a big part of me that didn't want you to know. I thought if I kept that part of my life from you it'd simply go away, be forgotten. I hoped that focusing on the present would help me forget," he softly explained. They stepped apart still holding hands, still embraced within each other's eyes.

"Every time you were about to uncover a part of my past, I felt the urge to walk away. Voices inside told me to tell you, especially when you had such a hard time sharing your past about Sean. I wanted to let you know we both had painful pasts, but I felt free without you knowing. I realize now, the past kept me a prisoner. I've needed you all along to help set me free. I guess I could say, you were my sign, I just never noticed. Does that make sense?"

She wanted to know the story behind every medal, from the most minor accomplishment to every detail leading to his Soldier's Medal, but she didn't want to stop his rushing thoughts or leave his warm embrace. Emotions stirred.

"Neither of us can keep our past locked inside a drawer, in a place where it keeps us from sharing who we really are and how we feel. If we're going to move forward, Ken, we have to make the past a part of our present."

Her eyes remained fixed on his. "I want to know everything there is about you, Mr. Ken Kavanaugh, from the moment you could talk, to every road, field, and valley that finally led you home."

"Hmm, I was told once to listen to my heart, for it would always lead me home," he thoughtfully said. "It finally makes sense now."

"What?" She felt a jolt of recognition. "Say that again," she commanded, studying his face intently.

"Oh, it's a saying someone gave me. It's on the little pillow over there on the couch."

She glanced at the leather sofa that stretched along the far wall of the living room and cautiously meandered closer. Her heart was pounding.

"Emmy, what's wrong? What is it?"

The sun had completely lowered and was now replaced by a full moon whose beams shone brightly into the room, creating a soft and natural light.

Her mouth was dry; her pulse raced. She glanced at Ken and back to the pillow. It was ivory and softly quilted with a flimsy ruffled border. Something was written in light blue, stitched across the middle. She cleared her throat.

"The pillow is beautiful, Ken. I love the saying, may I ask where you got it?" hardly daring to guess the answer.

Ken came to her side, bent down, and gently picked up the small pillow, handling it as though made of glass. He held it in the palms of his strong, callused hands. She sensed the pillow was special to him.

"I was coming home from Nam after I was dischar...after I was released. I had done some extended traveling in Europe to help clear my mind. I think it was the last train from Chicago. I was dog tired. Still confused, I really didn't want to come home, but didn't have anywhere else to go. I found my reserved seat and sat down across from an older woman, nice lady, grandma type. It was quiet for a while, and then she asked me questions about where I'd been and traveled.

"As I babbled on and on, she had a concerned and genuine look of interest in what I told her. I ended up talking the entire ride home. When we reached the end, I found out she had me pegged all along. I'll never forget her asking me, 'Did I choose to travel alone or had I traveled to be left alone?'

"Now, how did she ever pick up on that after the short amount of time we talked? Anyway, right before our final stop, she handed me this pillow. Guess she collects them and gives them to people. I clammed up on her pretty bad, didn't want to accept it. I hardly knew her, yet here she offered me this gift. She insisted and told me to keep the pillow for my own. Guess she saw something in me—probably the pain, so I finally obliged. It wasn't until I got off the train that I read the pillow's inscription."

She glanced down at the pillow and quietly read aloud, "Listen to your heart, for it will always lead you home."

"You know, she was right, it did," Ken acknowledged.

Tears welled up in her eyes and streamed down her cheeks. This was the sign she needed—the sign she'd been waiting for so long. She took Ken's hands in hers and slowly brought him to her. He smiled quizzically, not understanding her tears, but eager to wrap her in his warm embrace. She welcomed his strong hands as he pulled her closer. Their lips found each other's touch.

You've found your peace, Emmy. Heaven is here now also.

"Well, that settles it. I'm going to have to start collecting pillows." His smile reflected the warmth they'd shared.

She smiled back at him, happiness shining in her eyes as they continued to hold each other's embrace.

"I'm hoping those are happy tears, Emmy. What's with my pillow? Why did it touch you so?" he asked as he tilted his head to one side. Their eyes locked.

"Do you know the woman I met on the train?"

She was filled with emotion, barely able to speak. The sign she had waited for was purposely left for her to find. She slid her arms from around his neck to tightly grasp his hands. Envisioning the joy their future held, she quietly replied,

"She's my mother."

CHAPTER 20

Remember the Sunsets.

It was early Sunday evening. Grandma Rosie scurried about the kitchen getting dinner together so it was ready when Emmy and Joy returned home. Her train had returned safely from the shopping trip to Chicago, and she was thankful Gert's son, Hank, gave her a ride home. Her girls would be tired from the weekend and although they usually saved Sunday night for popcorn, she thought a bowl of hot homemade soup would warm them up after their weekend in the cool country air.

While she gave one last final stir to the soup, car doors slammed outside in the driveway. She pleasantly surprised when she peeked out the kitchen window. Emmy was walking with a nice looking familiar gentleman down the sidewalk towards the house.

He carried Joy who was snuggled sound asleep in his arms. She quickly untied her apron, draped it over the back of the kitchen chair, and walked over to the back porch to greet them. She held the door open as they quietly walked in. Emmy kissed her on the cheek and slipped past. She caught Ken's smile and wink when he made his way past her through the kitchen.

"She's exhausted. Running her up to bed and we'll be right back," Emmy whispered.

"Take your time, Dearie, take your time."

She gathered silverware hoping Ken would stay for dinner. After all, it was the least she could do after the weekend of entertainment he provided for her girls at the lake. Holding the sets of silverware in her hand, she paused and smiled. She was excited to chat with her old friend again and hear the rest of his story. Quickly setting the silverware down on the table, she turned to find Emmy behind her, Ken by her side.

"Mom, to my surprise, I believe you two have already met and we'll talk about that later, but I'd like to officially introduce you to my friend Ken—Ken Kavanaugh."

The sparkle had finally returned in her daughter's eyes—a radiant gleam she hadn't seen since the days before Sean had died. Ken had brought Emmy back to life.

She slowly made her way over to Ken who stood motionless, perhaps wondering if his encounters with her daughter these past few months had been her plan all along.

"So, young man, you finally found your way home." She took both his hands and recalled their large size and strength.

"I believe I have, Ma'am."

"We have a lot of catching up to do, you and I." She gazed at him as an old friend, eager to hear his latest adventures.

He slowly brought her hand to his lips and placed a soft kiss. "May I begin with, it's an honor to officially meet you," he said, as he gave a gentleman's bow.

His eyes were bluer than she remembered many months before when they traveled southbound on the City of New Orleans. The strong features of his face had finally found their one lacking element—a smile.

"The honor is all mine young man, all mine," she quickly responded.

She caught Emmy's glance and her beaming smile, as though touched by the special moment between her mother and friend.

How she had prayed for this moment for Emmy and now, it finally had come. Silence and smiles encompassed the small kitchen that smelled of freshly made chicken soup.

"You can stay for dinner, I hope? I want to hear all about your weekend adventure."

"I can't think of anywhere I'd rather be right now than with the two of you. But I must warn you, I'm starved." Ken chuckled, took a step back and held Emmy's arm.

"The soup smells wonderful, Mom. I'll get the crackers." Emmy added.

"I made a new one. Got the recipe from Hank, you know, Gert's youngest boy. He just returned from the Philippines, a Major in the Navy. It's called military chicken soup and you can eat up. It makes enough to feed an Army," she exclaimed holding up the old wooden spoon. Grandma Rosie stirred the pot. The soup thickened after she added her final ingredients of garlic, cilantro, and laurel leaves.

~ ~ ~

Emmy gathered three bowls and silverware from the kitchen table and strolled into the dining room. She set them at the long table that stretched from one end to the other.

Emmy loved this room bordered with deep mahogany wood and arched doorways. The paint on the stucco walls was light peach and a small ledge wound its way beneath the border of the ceiling. The ledge held a variety of ceramic knick-knacks including various ballerinas, 18th century dancers, and an assortment of decorative miniature plates.

She bent down and pulled out a fresh bottle of Sterling Cabernet from the wine rack that lay tucked beneath the buffet. When her body lowered, a white mosaic chevron framed picture was revealed. The picture was of a man in his twenties with sandy brown, curly hair wearing a yellow collared golf shirt. He sat in an oversized armchair and wore a large smile while cradling a newborn baby.

"That picture was taken the day we brought Joy home from the hospital. Sean was never more proud. He was so looking forward to being a father," she smiled in remembrance.

She stood up holding the bottle of wine. Ken's eyes traveled down the top of the buffet where two additional framed photos were perched. The first one was a family picture taken outside in front of the old oak tree.

"This must be you and Sean with your mom? You all look so happy, content."

Even though she noticed the pictures every day, right now they took on new meaning. Ken was different than Sean in so many ways and yet they shared one special quality, one that mattered to her the most—the ability to make her laugh.

Ken picked up the third picture from the end of the buffet. "Beautiful, Emmy. Where was this sunset taken?"

"From the balcony at the club where Sean worked. It overlooks the 18th green. Before Joy was born, Sean and I would often meet there after work for a cold beer or glass of wine. We'd sit for hours sharing our hopes and dreams for the future. We were so young, Ken. Joy wasn't even a sparkle in our eyes. This photo actually has a very special story if you'd like to hear."

She took in a deep breath and slowly let it out. It was the first time she'd felt like opening up to another man about Sean. She yearned to tell him more and was relieved by his quick response.

"Please, I want to hear anything you're willing to share."

"Okay. Well, we were relaxed sipping our wine, soaking in the beautiful, peaceful view. Sean got up to see if he could borrow the club's new instamatic camera to take a picture." She pointed to the photo. "This is the picture of the sunset that evening. We sat side by side watching the sun slowly go down deeper behind the clouds. As it lowered beneath the horizon, an unusual chill filled the air. I moved closer to Sean. He wrapped his arm around me, held me close and whispered, '*remember the sunsets*'.

"The prism of colors disappeared into the night's grasp. For a long time after he died, I couldn't watch a sunset without thinking about what he told me, wondering if he somehow knew or perhaps why he...."

Her voice broke. She closed her moist eyes and lowered her head. She wanted to embrace that moment, yet share Sean's memory.

"...I mean, you can always watch a sunset, right?" she added lightheartedly.

She recalled Ken mentioned he loved to sit on his pavilion and witness his private kaleidoscope of colors twirl and set before him.

"I wanted to share this story with you our first night out on your pavilion but it was too soon; we were just beginning to know each other.

"After Sean died, his phrase took on new meaning. With every sunset he talks to me, reminds me to never take any moment or the simplest things in life for granted. We do that with sunsets, life, with people we love. Sean always reminds me that with every sunset...." she paused, her voice quivered.

"There is also a sunrise," Ken added and took her hands. Slowly Ken brought her closer into his arms and held her. She snuggled into his soft blue sweater, returning his embrace. She was safe and happy swaddled in his arms. Together they would heal past wounds and finally begin to live forward.

A cough sounded behind them that came from the kitchen doorway. Her mother leaned on the doorway's frame and stared.

"You two 'bout done? I already called you twice from the kitchen. Soups on, Dearies, pick up your bowls and get it while it's hot."

She laughed. Her mother's smile indicated she hadn't minded waiting one bit.

Following orders, they filled their bowls with steaming delicious military chicken soup. Grandma Rosie grabbed the crackers and followed them back into the dining room.

Ken opened the wine and filled three glasses.

Grandma Rosie raised her glass. "Before I begin my toast, I have to ask, just how did you two Dearies finally figure it all out, hmm?" She lowered her glass and waited.

"I guess you could say our story actually began with the gift of a special pillow," Ken answered with a wink.

"And ended with a *deer* friend we'll soon never forget." She and Ken shared a knowing glance.

In unison, they raised their glasses to the center, the sound of each clink resounding throughout the room.

Grandma Rosie smiled and made her toast, "Here's to a new beginning that I pray someday leads to a very special union."

EPILOGUE

A child's purity simply sees what can be; and it is.

"Do you think Mommy will get married someday, Grandma Rothie?" Joy inquired. It was a week after the New Year. Grandma Rosie was packing for her long train ride to Arizona to visit her sister, Lelia, for the rest of the winter and into spring.

Joy sat on the edge of the high double-poster bed. Her tiny legs swung out and back knocking against the bed frame. She knew Joy was sad she was leaving and bet she was trying to think of questions hoping to delay her departure.

She calmly packed even though the sound of Joy's heels hitting the baseboard gave her an unwanted headache. She opened her closet door and stared at her clothes trying to decide what she absolutely needed and what could be left behind.

"I mean, if they get married Mommy would alwayth have someone to be with, right? I would jutht have me, now that you're leaving, right?"

The kicking stopped. She turned. Joy was holding the pillow she'd given her before her first day of kindergarten. She fought the tears slowly swelling in her eyes.

"I've tried to keep it white Grandma Rothie, just for you," Joy softly uttered while she studied the pillow.

She shuffled over to the bed and sat next to Joy's small frame, cuddling and holding her tight.

"First of all, Ken is a wonderful man and cares about both of you very much. I'm happy for you and your mom. I can't predict what the future will bring anymore than you'll be able to truly keep your pillow white. But always remember, my little Dearie, even blemishes get makeup."

Joy smiled up at her and snuggled in closer.

"If one happens to appear one day on your special pillow, all I ask is you learn from your mistake and become stronger from the experience. That's what your mom and Ken did, right? They were friends first and in time learned to love each other. I know Ken loves you, but it takes time to become a family, Dearie. Me being away for a while allows the three of you a chance to get used to each other, to see if together you'll make a great 'three family'. I personally have great hopes you will, but that's up to you, your mother, and Ken."

She kissed Joy softly on her forehead and continued packing. She wouldn't need her old flannel bathrobe, but couldn't depart from its comfort either. She unhooked it from behind the closet door, folded and lay it in her brown leather suitcase.

Joy plopped herself back on the bed holding her pillow across her stomach and stared at the ceiling. The silence in the room allowed the resonance from the ticking cat's eyes to amplify from over on the dresser.

"Do you think you'll get married again someday, Grandma Rothie, or do you think you're too old? I think I'd like having a Grandpa," Joy added with a smile.

She added her braided moccasins, tennis shoes, and two pairs of dress shoes to the overpacked suitcase laughing at the thought.

"You would, would you? Sounds like trouble to me, and yes, you're right, I am too old." Shaking her head, she laughed. She placed a jar of night cream, a package of hairnets, comb, and soft brush into her light blue overnight case with its clear plastic carrying handle.

"I know who you could marry, Grandma Rothie!" Joy suddenly sat up.

"Harry," she exclaimed loud and clear, hardly able to contain her excitement.

She dropped the hand mirror she was placing in her overnight case on the beige shag carpeted floor. She quickly picked it up delighted it was still intact.

"Harry would be a great grandpa, and I could ride and help him do his milk route in the thummers. You could live here all the time and Aunt Lelia could come and visit you in the winter, it'th a match made in heaven, Grandma Rothie."

She sat down on the edge of the bed knowing Joy's exciting idea still swarmed within her.

"Joy, I explained why it's important for me to stay a few months with Aunt Lelia. It doesn't mean I won't miss you terribly because quite honestly, I will. You know I will."

Joy curled her hair around her finger in front of her, something she did when she contemplated what she was going to say next. "Are you thaying you won't even go on a date with Harry?"

"No, Joy, Harry and I will always just be, well, acquaintances. I have enough love in my world right here with you and your mother. I'll be back to stay in a few months just as your sunflowers are beginning to grow. Why by that time you'll have grown almost as tall. We'll pick up just where we left off except this time you'll have quite a bit more to catch me up on about your mom and Ken.

"I can already see you sneaking down the stairs in the early morning and walking along the long dark hallway to my room. You'll slowly creep open the door to see if I'm awake, and...."

The bedroom door crept open, as if a ghost had been listening and entered the room. She stopped talking. They turned to see who or what was at the door—a familiar voice finished her sentence.

"... run around and jump into the bed!"

Emmy slithered through the bedroom doorway, ran around and jumped onto the bed. Joy screamed and held on to her arm for safety. The eruption of screams and laughter filled the room once more until the three giggled themselves to tears.

She was going to miss them. She always did, but after this particular visit, more than ever.

~ ~ ~

"All aboard, destination Chicago, IL!"

The train whistle sounded as Emmy, Joy, and Ken stood inside the warmth of the Cherry Grove train station to say their goodbyes. Ken had driven them early and taken care of her luggage. He made sure she was checked in all the way to Arizona, and confirmed her seat and berth were satisfactory.

"I can't thank you enough, Ken, for all your help. It certainly has been nice to have a young man around to take care of getting this old gal checked and ready to go."

His face, especially his eyes, appeared rejuvenated, not sorrowful and hard as when they first met. The mask he tried hard to hide behind had finally been thrown away.

Ken's concern for Emmy, Joy, and even herself was truly heartfelt. His sincerity ran deep and the outpouring of love and affection shown to her daughter and granddaughter was overwhelming. For the first time in many years, she was leaving her girls in good hands—strong callused hands. She was content in the journeys that lay ahead for everyone.

"You're welcome; it's truly been my pleasure. I'll take care of your girls, don't worry."

Ken gave her a tight hug, one that lingered. Neither wanted to let go. He stepped away to make room for Emmy and Joy to give their goodbyes.

"I'll miss you, Mom. Thank you for being here and for being you, you'll always be my rock. I love you. Tell Aunt Lelia hello for us and we'll see you in June."

Emmy stepped away. Joy ran into her open arms. She stooped to her knees for the sadly anticipated embrace.

Two small hands clasped themselves around her neck. No words were uttered—no words could be uttered. The silence held sounds of sniffled noses as Ken handed each a tissue.

"My life's little Joy, always remember that for me. I love you, Dearie, tight, tight hugs." She could barely say the words. Goodbyes were never her strong suit, hellos were so much easier.

Joy's tight grip remained until she finally whispered into her ear, "Tighter oneth back, Grandma Rothie. I love you."

Emmy leaned down and took hold of her daughter's hand. They stood back to wave goodbye as she boarded the train, tears gently streaming down their faces. Ken gave Grandma Rosie his arm and helped her onto the train pointing out her seat. For a moment, they stood at the rear of the train's aisle. She glanced once more at her new friend from behind her wire-framed glasses and smiled.

"I believe we're back where we started," he said returning her smile.

She tightened her grip around his arm, as though reconfirming their friendship and how far they'd both traveled since they left the train the first time.

"I'll take care of both of them. No need to worry."

"I'm counting on it, son."

With a hug and kiss only a grandma can give, she slowly made her way down the train's aisle to where Ken had pointed and took her reserved seat. After placing her carryon bag underneath her seat and her rose embroidered pillow on her lap, she checked to see who sat across from her. He was an older gentleman, farmer type with a red flannel shirt, worn jeans, brown boots, and an unlit cigar hanging out the corner of his mouth.

"Goin' back home or for a visit?" he inquired, his deep scruffy voice echoed his attire.

"A visit, how about you?" She gave a courteous smile and turned to gaze out the window as the train began its departure.

"I'm on a business trip to Oklahoma to meet with some suppliers."

What type of businessman would be dressed in jeans and a flannel shirt? She quickly decided she wasn't here to judge—skepticism would make for too long of a train ride.

"Oh, I see. Do you work for a company around here?"

"Nope, help manage a restaurant a few miles outside of Cherry Grove."

"Excuse me, did you say a restaurant?"

"That's right, a restaurant, maybe you've heard of it, called *Trusty's*."

She chuckled. *So, Ken got me back after all and with my own piece of medicine. Now, how did he pick up on that after the few short months we've known each other?*

"You finding somethin' funny 'bout the name?"

"I'm sorry, I didn't mean to laugh. Yes, I've heard of *Trusty's*. In fact, I've heard some very good things about *Trusty's*."

The two continued talking and laughing while the train sped down the barren railroad tracks surrounded on each side by lime covered corn, wheat, and bean fields. The chugging of the engine kept beat throughout the afternoon as they shared stories of their late spouses, children, grandchildren, and their simple maturing hopes and dreams.

~ ~ ~

The scenery became lost against the night sky. Darkness settled beyond the disappearing sun.

And a fawn ran in the distance, seeking to be nurtured, aspiring to grow, hoping one day he too might become a prince.

CPSIA information can be obtained at www.ICGtesting.com
Printed in the USA
LVOW11s1029100515

437756LV00002B/2/P